P9-CQH-932

A TREASURY
of illustrated
ENCHANTING STORIES
for CHILDREN

Sandy Creek
NEW YORK

Contents

3 – The Wizard of Oz

Written by L. Frank Baum
Adapted by Ronne Randall
Illustrated by Liz Monahan

46 – A Little Princess

Written by Frances Hodgson Burnett
Adapted by Anne Rooney
Illustrated by David Shephard

90 – The Secret Garden

Written by Frances Hodgson Burnett
Adapted by Anne Rooney
Illustrated by Bruno Merz

134 – Heidi

Written by Johanna Spyri
Adapted by Ronne Randall
Illustrated by Iva Sasheva

The Wizard of Oz

Dorothy lived with her Uncle Henry and her Aunt Em on a farm in the middle of the great Kansas prairies. Uncle Henry and Aunt Em both worked hard all day. Their skin was the same tone of gray as the dry, sun-burnt prairies that surrounded them. They never laughed and hardly ever smiled.

Dorothy, however, laughed a lot—especially at her little dog, Toto, with his silky black fur and merry black eyes. Dorothy loved him, and they played together every day.

Today, though, a big storm—a tornado—was coming and Dorothy, Aunt Em, and Uncle Henry were rushing to get to the storm cellar under their farmhouse, where they would be safe.

Toto was very frightened, and just as Dorothy was about to climb down the rickety cellar steps, he jumped out of her arms and tried to hide. Dorothy ran after him.

"Dorothy!" Aunt Em called, holding the cellar door open. "Come quickly! Run!" Dorothy grabbed Toto and tried to follow her aunt. But the house began to tremble and shake, and Dorothy fell to the floor.

Then an amazing thing happened. The whole house lifted up into the air and spun around! Terrified, Dorothy held Toto tightly. Hours passed but the wind just kept wailing and the house kept whirling. Realizing there was nothing else to do but wait calmly, Dorothy crawled onto her bed and eventually fell asleep.

The Munchkins

A great jolt woke Dorothy. When she looked outside, she could hardly believe her eyes. This wasn't Kansas! She had landed in the midst of a beautiful country filled with green grass and fruit trees. Suddenly Dorothy saw some small people marching toward her.

"We, the Munchkins, welcome you to our land," said a man. "Thank you for killing our enemy."

"I haven't killed anyone!" Dorothy exclaimed.

"Your house did," said a woman. Sure enough, there were two feet sticking out from under Dorothy's house!

"I am the Good Witch of the North," said the woman. "The Wicked Witch of the East has been keeping the Munchkins as slaves, but you have freed them!"

"Have her Silver Shoes as your reward for saving us," said one of the Munchkins. "They are magical."

"You are in the Land of Oz," explained the Good Witch. "There is still one Wicked Witch left—the Wicked Witch of the West—but you will be safe here with us."

"Thank you," Dorothy said, "but I just want to go home to Aunt Em and Uncle Henry. They will be so worried about me." And she began to cry.

"Maybe the Great Oz can help you," said the Good Witch. "The Wizard is more powerful than any of us and lives in the Emerald City. It's a long journey but you just need to follow the Yellow Brick Road." The Witch pointed at the road and gave Dorothy a gentle kiss on the forehead for good luck.

Dorothy Meets the Scarecrow

Dorothy went into her house to collect food for the journey ahead. She changed into a clean dress and the Wicked Witch's Silver Shoes—they fit perfectly!

As Dorothy and Toto walked along the Yellow Brick Road, many Munchkins came out to bow to them. They knew Dorothy had saved them from slavery and they were very grateful. One of the Munchkins invited Dorothy to supper and to rest overnight in his home.

The next morning, as she and Toto continued on their journey, Dorothy stopped to rest beside a cornfield. A raggedy Scarecrow stood in the middle of the field.

As Dorothy gazed at the Scarecrow, she thought she saw it wink. Yes, it did. It winked! Then it spoke!

"Good day," he said. "Would you be so kind as to take this pole out of my back?"

"You spoke!" Dorothy said in surprise, as she walked over and lifted the Scarecrow off the pole.

"Thank you very much," he said. "Now, who are you, and where are you going?"

"My name is Dorothy and I am going to the Emerald City to ask the Wizard to send me back home to Kansas."

"Maybe the Wizard could give me some brains," said the Scarecrow. "My head is stuffed with straw. I would love to have some brains so people don't think I'm a fool."

"Why not come along too?" said Dorothy. The Scarecrow nodded and they set off.

A while later, the road became rough and uneven, with lots of holes and missing bricks. The farms were shabbier too, and with fewer fruit trees. The farther they went, the more dismal everything looked.

At lunchtime, Dorothy offered the Scarecrow some bread from her basket.

"No, thank you," he said politely. "I never get hungry. Besides, my mouth is only painted on."

The Scarecrow wanted to know all about Dorothy so she told him about Kansas, and life with Aunt Em and Uncle Henry and how she missed them terribly even though everything had been dull and gray.

The Scarecrow told her about his lonely life. At first the crows were scared of him but then an old crow came and sat on his shoulder. When the old crow realized the Scarecrow wasn't going to hurt him, he hopped down and started eating the corn. Soon a whole flock of crows came and joined him.

The old crow had told the Scarecrow that brains were the only thing worth having and he had longed for them ever since. Without them he felt like a fool and didn't think he was a very good Scarecrow.

Dorothy felt sorry for the Scarecrow, and hoped the Wizard would be able to help him.

They kept walking and toward evening they came to an empty cottage in the forest. Dorothy and Toto were both very tired, so they all went inside to rest.

The Tin Woodman

Back on the Yellow Brick Road, Dorothy heard a groan. Through the trees, she saw a man made entirely of tin, holding an axe. Dorothy and the Scarecrow stared in amazement, while Toto barked.

"I've been like this for a whole year," the man said in a creaking voice.

"How can we help you?" asked Dorothy.

"My joints have rusted and I can't move," the man explained. "There is an oil-can in the cottage."

Dorothy ran to get the can and oiled the Tin Woodman's rusty joints so he could move again.

"You have certainly saved my life," he said with a sigh of relief. "How did you happen to be here?"

"We are going to the Emerald City to see the Great Oz," said Dorothy. "I want him to send me back home and the Scarecrow wants to ask for some brains."

"Perhaps I could ask Oz for a heart!" the Tin Woodman said.

"I was once human, you see, and fell in love with a Munchkin girl. The girl's mother did not want me to marry her daughter, so she asked the Wicked Witch of the East turn me to tin and take away my heart. Before I lost my heart, I was the happiest man in the world!"

Dorothy and the Scarecrow were pleased to have the Tin Woodman for company, and he joined them on their journey to the Emerald City.

The Cowardly Lion

Dorothy and her friends continued through the forest. Dry branches and dead leaves covered the Yellow Brick Road, making it difficult to walk.

Every now and then they could hear wild animals growling, which made Dorothy's heart pound with fright. Toto stayed close beside her.

Suddenly a terrible roar came from among the trees, and a huge Lion bounded out onto the road. With one blow of his big paw, he sent the Scarecrow spinning, and with another he knocked over the Tin Woodman. Toto ran at the Lion, barking loudly, and he opened his mouth to bite the little dog.

"Don't you dare bite Toto!" cried Dorothy, slapping the Lion on the nose. "You should be ashamed of yourself. You're just a great big coward!"

To Dorothy's surprise, the Cowardly Lion hung his head. "You're right," he said. "I know that when I roar everyone gets frightened, but the truth is, whenever there is danger, my heart beats faster because I am scared."

"At least you have a heart!" said the Tin Woodman. "I am going to ask the Great Oz for one."

"And I for some brains," said the Scarecrow.

"Do you think the Great Oz could give me courage?" asked the Cowardly Lion.

"Just as easily as he can send me back to Kansas," said Dorothy. "You are welcome to join us. By roaring you can scare away any wild beasts that come near."

That night, Dorothy and her friends camped out in the forest. All of Dorothy's bread was gone, so there was nothing for supper.

"I will kill a deer if you wish," the Cowardly Lion offered. "Then we would have some meat."

The Tin Woodman begged the Lion not to kill any animals. "It would make me cry to see a helpless deer get hurt," he said, "and the tears would rust my jaw."

The Scarecrow gathered some nuts and filled Dorothy's basket so she would not go hungry.

The next day the Yellow Brick Road went through a dark, gloomy part of the forest.

"The Kalidahs live here," the Lion whispered. "They are monstrous beasts with bodies like bears, heads like tigers, and long, sharp claws. I'm terrified of them!"

They walked on carefully, but had to stop when they came to a wide, deep ditch. How would they get across?

"I know!" said the Scarecrow. "If the Tin Woodman chops down that tree, it will make a bridge for us."

The Woodman got to work at once, and the tree soon fell with a crash. Just then they heard a loud growl.

"It's a Kalidah!" cried the Scarecrow. "Run!"

They raced to the other side of the ditch and the Tin Woodman chopped away at the tree trunk. Just in time, it fell into the ditch, taking the Kalidah with it. They were all safe!

The Deadly Poppy Field

The next morning the travelers came to a wide river at the edge of the forest. The Yellow Brick Road continued on the other side, where there were green meadows, flowers, and fruit trees.

The Tin Woodman made a raft to carry them across the river, and they all climbed aboard. But the current in the middle of the river was so strong that it sent them rushing downstream. They could not get to the other side.

"I will swim to shore," said the Cowardly Lion, "and pull the raft along with me."

When they were finally back on land, they realized the current had pushed them far from the Yellow Brick Road. As they walked back along the riverbank, they passed a meadow full of bright red poppies.

"Aren't they beautiful!" said Dorothy. Suddenly Dorothy felt so drowsy that she lay down and went to sleep right there by the side of the field. Toto fell asleep beside her. A moment later, the Lion fell asleep too. Only the Scarecrow and the Tin Woodman stayed awake, because they could not smell anything.

"We have to get our friends away from here!" said the Tin Woodman. "These poppies are deadly. Their fragrance sends people and animals to sleep. If they stay here, they will sleep forever!"

The Lion was too heavy to lift, but together they managed to carry Dorothy and Toto away from the field. Would a fresh breeze wake them up?

While they watched over Dorothy and Toto, the Tin Woodman and the Scarecrow saw a fierce wildcat chasing a little brown field mouse.

The Tin Woodman felt sorry for the little mouse, so he raised his axe to frighten the wildcat away. The field mouse was very grateful.

"I am the Queen of the Field Mice," she said, "and in return for saving my life, we field mice will do anything you ask."

The Tin Woodman and the Scarecrow asked if the mice could help rescue their friend the Lion. The mice squealed in terror but the Tin Woodman assured them that he was a Cowardly Lion who wouldn't hurt them, so they agreed to help.

The Tin Woodman chopped some wood to make a wagon, while the mice fetched string.

The Woodman used the string to harness the mice to the wagon, and they pulled it to the poppy field. They all helped to lift the Lion into the wagon. Then, with everyone's help, they rolled the wagon back to Dorothy, who was now awake.

"Thank you so much for saving my friend the Lion," Dorothy said.

"If you ever need us again, just whistle," said the Queen Field Mouse, handing Dorothy a tiny whistle.

To the Emerald City

When Dorothy and her friends set off again, they saw that all the houses near the Yellow Brick Road were painted green. The people were dressed in green as well.

"We must be getting near the Emerald City," said Dorothy, "for everything is green."

By evening they were hungry and tired, so they knocked on a farmhouse door. The owner invited them to have supper with her family. They were amazed when Dorothy told them they were going to see the Wizard of Oz.

"The Great Oz never lets anyone see him," said the woman's husband. "No one knows what he looks like."

"But we must see him," said Dorothy, "otherwise our whole journey will have been for nothing."

They stayed at the farmhouse that night. The next morning the travelers thanked the family and set off again. They soon reached the wall surrounding the Emerald City, where a little man stood guard at the gate. He was dressed head to toe in green.

"We have come to see the Wizard," said Dorothy.

The man was astonished.

"It is many years since anyone has dared ask to see the Great Oz," he said. "But since I am the Guardian of the Gate, I must take you to him. First, though, you must put on these special spectacles. You must wear these day and night," he warned them. "Otherwise you will be blinded by the brightness of the Emerald City."

The Guardian took the four friends to the Wizard's palace. The soldier who let them in said that the Wizard would see them, but on their own and only one each day.

Dorothy went in first. The walls, floor, and ceiling of the throne room were covered with sparkling emeralds. A green marble throne sat in the middle of the room, and on it sat a giant head, with no arms, no legs…and no body! Just a head!

"I am Oz, the Great and Terrible," said a booming voice. "Who are you, and why do you seek me?"

"Please," said Dorothy, "can you send me back to Kansas, where my Aunt Em and Uncle Henry are?"

"I will help you," said the Wizard, "but first you must help me and kill the Wicked Witch of the West!"

Dorothy burst into tears. "But I am just a little girl," she said. "I can't kill anyone, especially not a witch!"

The next day it was the Scarecrow's turn. This time there was a beautiful woman on the glittering throne. She told the Scarecrow that if he wanted a brain, he would have to kill the Wicked Witch of the West first.

To the Tin Woodman the Wizard took the shape of a terrible beast, and to the Lion he appeared as a fierce ball of fire. But his request was always the same: kill the Wicked Witch. After much discussion and many tears from Dorothy, the four friends agreed there was only one thing to do. They must destroy the Witch.

The Journey to the West

The Guardian of the Gate showed Dorothy and her friends which way was West. Soon they had left the Emerald City far behind, and were in the rough, hilly country of the West.

The Wicked Witch of the West had only one eye, but that eye was like a telescope and could see everywhere. When she saw Dorothy and her friends on her land, she was furious, and set out to destroy them.

First she summoned a pack of wolves by blowing on a silver whistle around her neck.

"Tear those strangers to pieces!" she ordered.
The wolves attacked, but luckily the Tin Woodman saw them coming. He chopped off the wolves' heads one by one with his axe.

Next, the Wicked Witch ordered a flock of crows to peck out their eyes. But the crows were frightened by the Scarecrow and flew away.

The Witch, angrier than ever, sent out a swarm of bees to sting Dorothy and her friends to death. The Scarecrow saw the bees approaching and had an idea. He told the Tin Woodman to take out his straw so Dorothy, Toto, and the Lion could hide underneath it. When the bees arrived, the Tin Woodman was the only one they could sting and they soon broke their sharp stings on his hard metal shell.

They all helped stuff the Scarecrow's straw back into his clothes, and set off once again.

The Winged Monkeys

The Witch had only one thing left to use. She put on her Golden Cap and called her most powerful helpers, the Winged Monkeys. She could only call on them three times, and this would be the third time.

When the Monkeys arrived, the Witch said, "Destroy them all except the Lion. I will hold him prisoner."

The Monkeys caught the Tin Woodman first. Lifting him high, they dropped him on some rocks, where his body lay battered and broken. They caught the Scarecrow next and took out all his stuffing. Then they tied up the Lion and flew him back to the Witch's courtyard. But when they saw the mark of the Good Witch's kiss on Dorothy's forehead, they dared not harm her. Instead they took her to the Witch.

The Witch was also afraid of the mark and of the Silver Shoes, but she soon realized that Dorothy was unaware of their magic powers. She decided to make Dorothy her slave and find a way to steal them.

Dorothy worked hard, sweeping and scrubbing, and began to fear she would never make it home. One day, in an attempt to snatch the shoes, the Witch tricked Dorothy into tripping. This made Dorothy so angry that she flung a bucket of water at the Witch.

Then an amazing thing happened: the Wicked Witch of the West melted away, leaving only a puddle behind!

The Rescue

After mopping up the puddle, Dorothy rushed to the courtyard to free the Lion. Then they called all the Witch's slaves together to tell them that they were also free. They were called the Winkies, and the land had been theirs before the Wicked Witch had captured them.

"If only the Scarecrow and the Tin Woodman were with us," said the Lion, "I would be so happy!"

"We'll help you find them!" said the Winkies. They formed a search party and quickly found the Tin Woodman's broken body. Tenderly, they carried him back to the Witch's castle where Dorothy and the Lion were anxiously waiting.

The Winkies' best tinsmiths repaired the Tin Woodman's body, and they fashioned a brand-new axe for him of shimmering gold and silver. They found the Scarecrow's clothes, which they stuffed with fresh, clean straw. The two friends were both as good as new!

It was time for Dorothy and her friends to go back to the Emerald City and tell the Great Wizard that they had done what he'd asked. The Winkies wished them well, and gave them presents for their journey: golden collars for Toto and the Lion; a sparkling bracelet for Dorothy; a silver oil-can for the Tin Woodman; and a gold-headed walking stick for the Scarecrow.

Dorothy went to the kitchen to get some food for the journey. There she also found the Witch's Golden Cap.

"That looks pretty," she said. "I think I'll wear it."

There was no Yellow Brick Road to lead them from the Witch's castle back to the Emerald City. The travelers had to find their way through fields of wild flowers, and before long they were lost.

They wandered for days, sleeping under the stars, hoping to see something that would show them the way. Finally, too exhausted to go any farther, they sat down on the grass.

"Do you think the Field Mice know the way to the Emerald City?" Dorothy wondered.

She blew her whistle and within minutes there was the patter of tiny feet. Soon they were surrounded by little brown mice.

"Can you tell us the way to the Emerald City?" Dorothy asked them.

The Queen stepped forward. "Of course," she said. "But it is far away. The Witch's Golden Cap gives its wearer three wishes. Summon the Winged Monkeys, and they will help you."

When Dorothy realized that the Golden Cap was more than just a pretty hat, she was doubly glad she had taken it. Dorothy called for the Monkeys. They arrived very quickly and agreed to Dorothy's request. Holding the four friends in their arms, the Monkeys rose into the air and flew off. Very soon they were all in the Emerald City.

The Discovery of Oz, the Terrible

After a long wait at the Wizard's palace, the soldier finally took them into the Throne Room. A booming voice said: "I am Oz, the Great and Terrible. Why do you seek me?"

"The Wicked Witch is dead," said Dorothy. "Now you must keep your promises."

"Er…come back tomorrow," said the Voice, a little shakily.

"Don't make us wait!" roared the Lion, so loudly that Toto jumped, knocking over a screen. To everyone's amazement a little old man stood there, shaking.

"Who are you?" asked Dorothy in surprise.

"I am Oz, the Great and Terrible," said the man, with a sheepish look. "But you can call me Oz. As you can see, I am not a Wizard at all. I am a just a common man."

"You mean you've been fooling us all along?" Dorothy asked.

"Yes," admitted Oz guiltily. "I was once a magician so I know how to do lots of tricks. The Emerald City isn't even green. It just looks that way through the glasses. I used to fly hot-air balloons and when the people saw me coming through the clouds, they thought I was a great Wizard. Please don't reveal my secret."

"But how will you keep your promises to us?" asked the Scarecrow.

"Come back tomorrow and I will do my best," said Oz.

Oz Keeps his Promise

The next day, the Scarecrow was the first to go in to see Oz. He was very eager to get his brains.

"I will have to remove your head," said Oz, "but I will put it back again, and it will be better than before."

He took off the Scarecrow's head and replaced the straw with bran. When he put it back on the Scarecrow, he said, "Now you have fine bran-new brains."

"Thank you so much!" said the Scarecrow. He rushed out to tell his friends how much wiser he felt.

Next, it was the Tin Woodman's turn to get his heart. Oz opened a drawer and took out a lovely red velvet heart stuffed with sawdust.

"Is it a kind heart?" asked the Tin Woodman.

"Very," said Oz and he cut a small hole in the Tin Woodman's chest, just big enough to hold the new heart.

When the Lion came in, Oz took a green bottle down from the shelf and poured some liquid into a bowl.

"Drink that," he told the Lion.

"What is it?" asked the Lion.

"Well," said Oz, "if it were inside you, it would be courage—because courage always comes from the inside."

The Lion drank all the liquid, and said he felt very brave indeed. Oz was pleased with himself.

"How can I help playing tricks," he said to himself, "when everyone wants me to do things that can't be done? But there's still one problem: how can I get Dorothy back to Kansas?"

Dorothy was longing to go home, but Oz needed time to think. At last he sent for her.

"I have a plan," he said. "I came here in a balloon, and I'm sure we can leave in one. We can make one out of silk—there is plenty of silk in the palace. We'll fill it with hot air, and it will float us home."

"Us?" said Dorothy. "Are you coming with me?"

"Yes," replied Oz. "I am tired of being shut up in this palace. I can't go anywhere, because if I did, everyone would realize that I am not a real Wizard. I would much rather go back to Kansas with you and join the circus."

For the next three days, Dorothy helped Oz make the balloon. When it was finished, they attached a big clothes basket to it. Oz announced that he was going to visit a brother wizard who lived in the clouds, and that Dorothy was going with him. A big crowd came to see them off.

"While I am away," Oz announced, "the Scarecrow will rule over you. Obey him as you would me. Now come, Dorothy, climb into the basket."

The hot air was making the balloon rise and tug at its ropes, but Dorothy wouldn't leave without Toto who had chased a cat into the crowd.

Suddenly there was a loud SNAP! The balloon's ropes broke, and Oz went floating up into the sky. Dorothy watched helplessly as Oz and the balloon drifted off without her.

Setting Out for the South

Now that Oz was gone, Dorothy wondered how she would ever get back home. She used the Golden Cap to call the Winged Monkeys, but the Monkey King said they could not go to Kansas.

Dorothy didn't know what to do until a soldier in the Wizard's palace mentioned that Glinda, the Good Witch of the South who ruled over the Quadlings, might be able to help.

Dorothy and her friends set off for the South, and traveled for days. They went through a thick, dark wood, with frightening fighting trees. Then they climbed over a smooth, high wall and into a land where the ground was as white and shiny as a dinner plate, and the tiny people were made of fragile china.

In another forest, they came upon a crowd of noisy animals having a meeting. When the animals saw the Lion, they welcomed him.

"You have come just in time to save us from our enemy," they said. The enemy was a huge spider that crawled through the forest, eating animals great and small. Now full of courage, the Lion bravely crept up to the sleeping spider and, with one blow, knocked off its head!

"You need not worry about your enemy any more," he told the animals. All the beasts bowed to the Lion and said he was now their King. The Lion promised to come back and rule over them once Dorothy was on her way.

The Hammer-heads

After leaving the forest, the travelers came to a steep hill, covered from top to bottom with pieces of rock. As they began to climb, a huge hammer-shaped head popped up over a rock and said, "Keep back! This is our hill, and no one is allowed to cross it!"

"We're crossing this hill whether you like it or not," said the Scarecrow, moving forward boldly.

Quick as a flash, the huge head shot forward as its neck stretched out. It hit the Scarecrow hard, sending him tumbling down the hill. Laughter rang out around them, and suddenly hundreds more Hammer-heads appeared, one behind each rock. The Lion dashed up the hill, but before he could get very far, another head shot forward and sent him rolling backward.

"Fighting these horrid heads is useless," the Lion said as he got up.

"But how will we get over the hill?" Dorothy asked.

"Call the Winged Monkeys," said the Tin Woodman. "You still have one wish left."

So Dorothy put on the Golden Cap and sent for the Winged Monkeys. They were there in an instant and swiftly carried Dorothy and her friends south to Quadling country. The land seemed rich and happy, with fields of ripening grain and rippling brooks. All the fences, houses, and bridges were painted bright red. It seemed like a happy place.

Meeting Glinda the Good Witch

The travelers knocked on a farmhouse door and were welcomed in by the farmer's wife. She was kind and generous, and gave Dorothy and her friends a good dinner. Then she told them how to get to the castle of the Good Witch Glinda.

When they got to the castle, Glinda saw them at once. She was beautiful, with flowing red hair and kind blue eyes, and she sat on a throne of rubies.

Dorothy told Glinda everything that had happened, starting with the tornado.

"Of course I will help you," said Glinda. "But I will need the Golden Cap." Dorothy had already used its magic three times and so was happy to part with it. Glinda then told them how she would use her three commands.

"I will ask the Winged Monkeys to take the Scarecrow back to the Emerald City, where he will be a wonderful ruler," she said. "Tin Woodman, you shall go back to the Land of the Winkies, where you will be a wise and good-hearted ruler. Finally, the Winged Monkeys will take the Lion back to the forest, where he will be King of the Beasts."

"Then what will happen to the Golden Cap?" asked Dorothy.

"I will give it to the King of the Winged Monkeys," said Glinda. "Then he and his band will be freed from its power forever."

"But what about me?" wondered Dorothy.

Dorothy's Wish Is Granted

The Scarecrow, the Tin Woodman, and the Lion had had their wishes granted and would now be rulers of their own lands, but Dorothy was still puzzled.

"How will I get back to Kansas?" she asked.

"The Silver Shoes will take you there," Glinda replied. "If you had known their power, you could have gone home the first day you got here."

"But then I never would have got my brains!" said the Scarecrow.

"Nor I my heart!" said the Tin Woodman.

"And I would have been a coward forever," said the Lion.

"That is all true," said Dorothy. "I am glad that I have helped but now that you are all happy, what I want most of all is to go back to Kansas."

"The Silver Shoes have wonderful powers," said Glinda. "All you have to do is click your heels three times and tell the shoes where to take you."

So Dorothy would at last get her wish. She hugged and kissed each of her friends. They were all very sad to say goodbye—but they were happy for each other as well.

Glinda stepped down from her throne to give Dorothy a goodbye kiss. Then, taking Toto in her arms and saying one last farewell, Dorothy clicked her heels three times and said, "Take me home!"

Home Again

Instantly, Dorothy and Toto were lifted up and went whirling through the air. Everything was happening so quickly that all Dorothy could hear or feel was the wind rushing past her ears.

The Silver Shoes took just three steps, then stopped so suddenly that Dorothy found herself rolling over and over on the grass before she even knew where she was. Finally Dorothy sat up and looked around.

"Oh, good gracious!" she cried. For she could see that she was on the wide Kansas prairie. Right in front of her was a new farmhouse—the one that Uncle Henry built after the tornado carried off the old one. And there, milking the cows in the farmyard just as he always had, was Uncle Henry himself. Toto jumped out of Dorothy's arms and ran toward him, barking joyfully.

Dorothy stood up, wondering where the Silver Shoes had gone. At that moment, Aunt Em came out of the house, holding a watering can. When she saw Dorothy, she dropped the watering can and ran to her with her arms open wide.

"Oh, my darling child!" she cried, hugging Dorothy tightly and covering her face with kisses. "Where in the world have you been?"

Dorothy thought her heart would burst with happiness.

"I've been in the Land of Oz," she replied. "Oh, Aunt Em, I'm so happy to be home!"

THE END

A Little Princess

Sara Crewe had just arrived from India. She leaned her head against her father's shoulder as their carriage clattered through the London streets. The yellow fog hanging over London made the day as dark as night. She was shocked at the contrast between the hot country she had known all her life and the cold one she had come to.

"Papa," she said. "Is this the place?"

"Yes, little Sara," he answered. "It is."

Sara's mother had died when Sara was born, and she had always lived with her father. Sara had known that she would be sent to school in England when she was old enough. And, at seven, she finally was.

They drew up in front of a big, dull house with a brass plate that read, "Miss Minchin, School for Young Ladies". Captain Crewe lifted his daughter from the carriage and they went inside.

"I don't like it, Papa," Sara said. Everything was square, hard, ugly, and unfriendly. When Miss Minchin came in, Sara felt she suited the house—she looked unfriendly, too.

"It will be wonderful to have such a beautiful and clever student," Miss Minchin said. Sara thought it was an odd thing to say, as she did not think herself beautiful and Miss Minchin did not yet know if she was clever.

Captain Crewe said that Sara was to have everything she wanted, including her own maid, carriage, fine clothes, and the best rooms.

Sara told Miss Minchin that her best friend would be Emily.

"Who is Emily?" Miss Minchin asked. Sara replied that Emily was the perfect doll, but she did not have her yet.

"What an original child," Miss Minchin said, smiling at her coldly.

Sara stayed with her father in his hotel while he was in London. Every day, they went shopping to buy her beautiful clothes with frills and furs and feathers. They went from shop to shop in search of Emily, until at last they found her. And then they bought Emily lots of lovely clothes, too.

On his last day, Captain Crewe took Sara back to Miss Minchin's and said goodbye. She sat at the window of her lovely rooms watching until his carriage was out of sight. Miss Minchin sent her sister, Miss Amelia, to see what Sara was doing. But she had locked the door.

"I want to be quite by myself, if you please," Sara said. Miss Minchin was relieved that Sara did not shout and cry as she had expected such a spoiled child to do. And, although she thought Sara's clothes ridiculous, she looked forward to showing her off as the richest pupil in school.

The other girls at the school had heard about Sara's arrival and there were rumors about her lovely clothes and luxurious rooms. They all turned to watch as she walked to her place on the first day of class.

Miss Minchin's School

Miss Minchin introduced Sara to the class and then said, "As your papa has employed a French maid for you, I expect he wants you to learn French." She gave Sara a very simple book of French words.

"I have not learned French, but…" Sara began. She wanted to explain that her mother had been French, but Miss Minchin stopped her.

"That is enough. It is time you began."

When the French teacher arrived, Miss Minchin told him Sara was reluctant. But Sara spoke to him quickly in perfectly fluent French.

"Ah, Madame," the teacher said to Miss Minchin. "There is not much I can teach her—she *is* French. Her accent is delightful."

Miss Minchin was furious that Sara had made her look foolish. From then onward, she didn't like Sara.

A sad-looking, plump girl called Ermengarde watched the drama unfold, anxiously chewing her pigtail. Miss Minchin soon told her off, and Sara felt sorry for her. She later learned that Ermengarde's father was always disappointed in her as she was not a quick learner. Sara promised to help her and Ermengarde cheered up.

"Is it true," Ermengarde asked, "that you have your own playroom?"

"Yes," said Sara. "I make up stories when I play, but I don't like people to hear."

Sara took Ermengarde to her room to meet Emily, whom Ermengarde thought the most beautiful doll she had ever seen. Sara told her she liked to imagine that when no one was around, dolls could move and talk and act just like little girls. Ermengarde spent the happiest hour of her entire life in Sara's room.

Sara was always kind and delightful and generous to everyone around her. But her good fortune annoyed two people. One was Miss Minchin, who thought her spoiled, but useful for showing off as a star pupil. The other was Lavinia, who was jealous of Sara. She had been Miss Minchin's favorite and the most popular girl in the school before Sara arrived.

The younger children especially loved Sara. She was kind about their troubles and tantrums.

"If you are four, you are four," she said to Lavinia, who had slapped little Lottie and called her a "brat". "But soon you will be too old for silly tantrums."

One day, Sara heard Miss Minchin and Miss Amelia trying to calm Lottie, who was wailing, "I haven't got a mamma!" The two women were cross and despairing in turn and it didn't help at all. Sara asked if she might try to calm Lottie. Instead of fussing, she sat quietly while Lottie cried. At last she told Lottie that she didn't have a mother either. She promised to be Lottie's mother while she was at school. Lottie quickly calmed down.

The Little Princess

Sara had been at Miss Minchin's school for two years when she caught sight of a dirty, smudgy face watching her as she went to her carriage dressed in her furs. That evening, she saw the very same girl come into the schoolroom carrying a box of coal. The tiny servant girl spent as long as she could making up the fire so that she could stay and listen as Sara told a story about a mermaid. All the girls, even Lavinia, could not help crowding around to listen to Sara's stories in the evenings. When Sara noticed the girl listening, she raised her voice so that the servant girl could hear more easily. All at once, the girl dropped a brush.

"That servant has been listening!" said Lavinia. But Sara did not mind at all. She believed that stories belonged to everyone.

Later Sara discovered from her maid, Mariette, that the little girl was Becky, the lowest servant in the house. Becky was always sent to run errands in the cold. She was always hungry and filthy from making up the fires.

A few weeks later, Sara came back from a dance class dressed in a rose pink dress with real matching roses in her hair. She opened the door to her room and found the little servant sleeping in a chair in front of the fire.

"Oh!" cried Sara, when she saw her. "You poor thing!"

Becky always saved cleaning Sara's room until last, as it was the prettiest and was full of lovely, interesting things. But today she was so exhausted that she had rested for a moment in Sara's soft, comfy chair—and then fallen fast asleep. When Becky opened her eyes, she saw Sara in her beautiful dress.

"Oh, Miss!" she cried, straightening her cap and jumping to her feet.

"I didn't mean to! The fire was so warm, and I was so cold and tired…"

Sara put a hand on her shoulder and laughed kindly.

"Ain't you very angry, Miss?" Becky asked, afraid that Sara would tell Miss Minchin.

"Why, no," Sara said. "We are just the same. I am only a little girl like you. It is just an accident that I am not you and you are not me!"

Becky did not really understand, but Sara sat her down, gave her some cake, and began to chatter to her.

Becky said Sara's dress made her look like a princess. Sara told her that she sometimes pretended to be a princess, and always tried to behave like one. Then she told her more of the mermaid story Becky had overheard. She promised to tell her a bit more of the story every day if Becky came to her room after she finished her work.

After Becky had gone, Sara murmured to herself, "If I were a real princess, I could give money and presents to everyone. As a pretend princess, I shall be kind to people instead."

Kind Deeds

A little time later, a letter came from Captain Crewe explaining that he was investing in some diamond mines with an old friend. It was going to make him very rich. Everyone in the school was excited, except for Lavinia and her friend Jessie. Lavinia didn't believe there were such things as diamond mines. Jessie told her that she'd heard Sara liked to pretend she was a princess, and they both laughed spitefully.

"I suppose she'd think she was a princess even if she were a beggar," Lavinia laughed. When Lavinia and Jessie mocked Sara, she told them that pretending to be a real princess helped her to be kind to people.

Sara saw Becky every day. She began to buy Becky treats to eat as she was always so thin and hungry. Slowly, Becky grew plumper, healthier, and happier. She was made to work harder as she grew stronger, but she felt she could put up with anything because she could look forward to spending time with Sara at the end of the day.

When it was nearly Sara's birthday, a letter came for her from her father. Captain Crewe was unwell, but he had sent instructions to Miss Minchin for Sara's birthday, and said that Sara must choose a doll. Sara said it would be her "Last Doll", as at eleven she was almost too big for dolls. Miss Minchin bought all the things that Captain Crewe asked for—the doll, fine clothes, and a birthday tea.

A Terrible Shock

When Sara's birthday arrived, the whole school went into Miss Minchin's sitting room for the tea party, and Miss Minchin made a speech about what a wonderful pupil Sara was. Miss Minchin saw Becky listening, and tried to send her away.

"Please may Becky stay?" Sara asked.

Miss Minchin was horrified.

"But she is a scullery maid!" she said. However, to please Sara, she let Becky stay.

Sara opened her presents. She had books, clothes, jewelry, and the beautiful new doll. But just then, Miss Amelia came in.

"Sara, your papa's lawyer has come to see Miss Minchin," she said, "so you must all run along."

Everyone rushed away, but Becky stayed to look at the presents a moment too long. Just as she was about to leave, Miss Minchin came in with the lawyer, Mr. Barrow. In a panic, Becky hid under a table, and from there she heard everything.

Mr. Barrow told Miss Minchin that the diamond mines had failed and Captain Crewe had lost all his money before he died.

"He died!" cried Miss Minchin.

"Yes. And he lost every penny he had. He was already ill with jungle fever when he heard the news about the diamond mines, and the shock killed him. Sara is left penniless, and in your care."

Miss Minchin turned white with rage.

"I have been robbed and cheated! I will turn her out to live in the street!" she shouted.

"I wouldn't do that, Madam," Mr. Barrow said. "It wouldn't look good for the school. Better keep her and make use of her as a servant."

Miss Minchin called Miss Amelia and told her to tell Sara the news and send her to put on a black dress. Then she sat and considered how much she had just spent on Sara's birthday—money that she would never be paid back. When Sara appeared in front of Miss Minchin a few hours later, her face was white with dark rings under her eyes. She had listened to the news from Miss Amelia without speaking, and then run to her room where she repeated over and over, "My papa is dead! My papa is dead!"

Now she stood, clutching Emily, as Miss Minchin told her she would have no time for dolls in the future. She would work as a servant and do everything she was told.

"You are a beggar now—not a princess!" Miss Minchin said. "You have no relations, no home, no one to care for you. You can stay here but you must work."

Sara ran from the room, but Miss Amelia stopped her from going into her own bedroom.

"This is not your room now. You must sleep in the attic next to Becky's room," she said.

A Strange New Life

As she closed the door behind her, Sara's heart sank. This was another world. The room had a slanting roof with a skylight, and the whitewash was peeling off the walls. There was nothing but a hard bed and a few pieces of battered furniture. Sara sat on a footstool, laid Emily over her lap, and cried.

After a short time, there was a tap at the door, and Becky came in. She too had been crying.

"Oh, Becky," Sara said. "I told you we were just the same. You see how true it is? I'm no princess any more."

"Yes, you are!" Becky cried. "Whatever happens to you, nothing could make you different!"

The first night Sara spent in the attic was a night she never forgot. She felt sadder than she had ever felt in her life. She tossed and turned, trying to get comfortable, and whispered over and over to herself, "My papa is dead!" The wind howled in the darkness and Sara heard shuffling and squeaking in the walls. She knew it was mice and rats. She lay trembling, with the covers pulled over her head.

Sara's life changed all at once. Her maid Mariette was sent away, and from the very next morning, Sara had to sit at breakfast with the smallest children and help them. She was sent on errands and had chores heaped on her by the servants, who rather enjoyed ordering around the girl they had been forced to make a fuss over before.

For the first few months, Sara thought that if she worked hard, the servants might be kinder to her. But she soon realized that this wasn't true—they simply gave her more tasks and scolded her. She no longer had lessons, but studied alone at the end of the day—she was afraid she would forget what she had learned if she did not study.

Miss Minchin didn't like Sara to talk to the other girls.

"To think that she was the girl with the diamond mines!" Lavinia scoffed. "Doesn't she look odd now!"

Sara worked harder than ever. She tramped through cold, wet streets carrying parcels, and grew shabbier and more miserable every day. She had to eat her meals downstairs with the servants. Although her heart was breaking, she told herself, "Soldiers don't complain, and I shall not. I shall pretend this is a war."

There were times when Sara thought her heart might break of loneliness if it were not for her few friends. Becky still helped Sara whenever she could. And, one day, Sara went up to her attic room at the end of the day and found Ermengarde there waiting for her. Ermengarde looked around the tiny, bare room.

"Oh Sara, how can you bear living here?" she asked, sorrowfully. Sara started to feel a little more like her old self as her imagination began to work.

"If I pretend it's quite different, I can," she said. "Or if I pretend it is a place in a story."

Melchisedec

Lottie was also a good friend to Sara. She was too small to understand what had happened and Sara didn't want to tell her. But, one day, Lottie climbed the stairs to Sara's room to find out for herself.

"Sara!" she cried, horrified that the room was so bare and ugly. Sara was worried that Lottie would make a fuss and be discovered.

"It's not so bad," she said quickly. "Look, you can see all sorts of things from the window." She showed Lottie the view from the skylight and a tiny sparrow hopping about. They fed some crumbs to the sparrow, and Sara helped her to imagine how lovely the room could be if there were a fire in the grate and comfortable furniture. When Lottie had gone, though, the room felt cold and empty again.

"It's sometimes the loneliest place in the world," Sara said to herself. At that moment, she heard a little sound, and looked up. There, sitting sniffing the air, was a large rat.

"I dare say it's rather hard to be a rat," Sara said. "Nobody likes you. But it's not your fault you were born a rat." She sat very still, and eventually the rat crept up and ate some of the crumbs that Lottie had dropped on the floor. Sara decided to call him Melchisedec and make him a friend.

"After all," she thought, "prisoners made friends with rats."

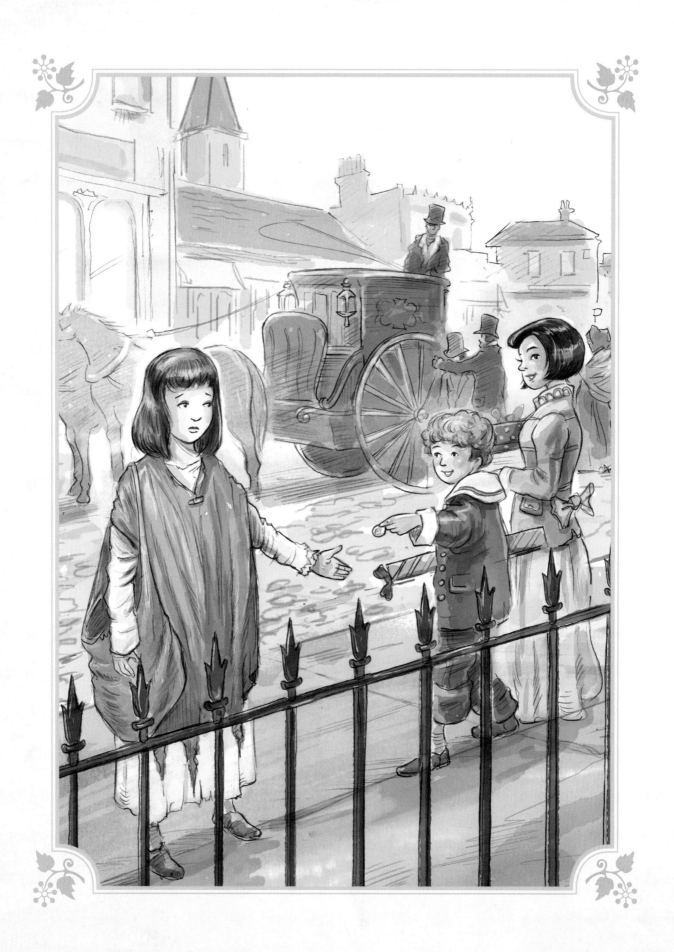

The Indian Gentleman

When Sara had been rich and finely dressed, everyone had admired her when she went out. Now, no one looked at her at all, and feeling invisible made her lonelier than ever. Instead, she watched other people. She liked to look into one nearby house in particular. It belonged to a family she called the Large Family, because there were eight children. One day, as she watched them get into their carriage, one of the boys turned toward her.

"Here, poor little girl, here's a sixpence for you."

Sara suddenly realized that she looked just like the poor children on the street. She didn't want to take the sixpence, but she saw it would make the boy happy, so she did. She thanked him so politely that the Large Family children were puzzled.

"She can't be a beggar," one of the girls said. They were so interested in her after that that they watched out for her, and called her "the little girl who is not a beggar". Sara made a hole in the sixpence and hung it around her neck.

The house next to Miss Minchin's had been empty for years. Sara longed for someone to move in. How nice it would be if a friendly head could pop out of the skylight next to hers and wish her good morning!

Then, one day, she saw men carrying crates and furniture into the house. Some of the furniture looked Indian. What a lovely sight!

That night, Becky came to Sara's room with news.

"It's an Indian gentleman," she said. "He's very rich, and he's ill, and the father of the Large Family is his lawyer!"

It was a few weeks before the Indian gentleman moved in. He had no wife or children, only a nurse and two servants. He looked sick, was very thin, and was always wrapped in furs.

Some time later, Sara was standing on the table looking at the sunset out of the skylight, when she saw a head at the next window. It was brown-skinned and wearing a turban. She smiled at the man, and he smiled back but, as he did so, he accidentally let go of a little monkey he was holding. It ran across the roof and jumped through Sara's skylight!

Sara had learned to speak Hindustani when she lived in India, and spoke it now to the man to ask if the monkey would let her catch him. The man was called Ram Dass and was the servant, or lascar, as they were sometimes known, of the Indian gentleman. They decided it would be best if he crawled across the roof and caught the monkey himself. Despite the shabby attic, Ram Dass treated Sara with all the respect she was used to from her servants in India.

After he had gone, she thought about what had happened. She straightened her thin little body, and said, "Even if I am dressed in rags and tatters, I can still be a princess inside."

The Other Side of the Wall

Sara grew fond of the new gentleman next door, even without meeting him. She learned that he was English, but had lived in India for a long time. He had fallen ill after some bad luck with diamond mines.

In turn, the gentleman, whose name was Mr. Carrisford, learned a little about Sara. The children of the Large Family told him about the "little girl who is not a beggar", and Ram Dass described the adventure with the monkey. He called his lawyer, the father of the Large Family, Mr. Carmichael, over for a talk.

"Hearing about the poor girl next door has made me worry that Crewe's child—the child I never stop thinking about—could be in a similar state," he said.

"If the child is in Paris, as you believe, I am sure she is well looked after," Mr. Carmichael replied.

"I am not *sure* she is in Paris!" he worried. "I only think that because her mother was a Frenchwoman. I *must* find her. Crewe was my oldest friend and his child might be begging in the street. He put every penny he had into the diamond mines, and he died thinking I had lost his money!"

"Come, come," Carmichael reassured him. "You were ill at the time, too, and could not tell him the mines had had a change of luck or ask about his daughter. We shall find the child and you will have a fortune to hand to her. I have a new lead. I will travel to Moscow and look for her there."

A Secret Feast

The winter was bleak, and Sara suffered cruelly. One day, she found a silver coin in the mud. Sara was hungrier than ever and crossed the road to the bakers. But, on the way, she spotted a beggar child with eyes even hungrier than her own. Sara bought six hot buns and gave five of the buns to the cold and starving child.

"She is hungrier than I am," she said to herself.

When she got home, she saw the children of the Large Family saying goodbye to Mr. Carmichael as he set off to travel to Russia.

"If you find the little girl, Father, give her our love," shouted one of them.

I wonder who the little girl is, thought Sara.

While Sara had been out, Mr. Carrisford had asked his secretary and Ram Dass to sneak across the roof and go into Sara's attic room. They measured, and took notes, and saw how shabby it was.

"Do you think it can be done while she sleeps?" the secretary asked Ram Dass.

"I can move as if my feet were velvet," he replied.

They slipped away, and when Sara returned that evening there was no sign they had ever been there. She was late for dinner, and the cook gave her a piece of stale bread. As Sara climbed the steps to the attic room, she saw a light under her door and found Ermengarde waiting for her. Sara was glad, but Ermengarde did not really understand how terrible Sara's life was.

As Sara and Ermengarde talked, they heard Miss Minchin shouting at Becky for stealing a meat pie. Becky was muttering that she hadn't stolen the pie, though she would have liked to—she was so hungry. Ermengarde opened her eyes wide in horror.

"Sara, are *you* ever hungry?"

Sara was just too tired to pretend.

"Yes," she said, "I'm so hungry now I could eat you!"

Ermengarde jumped up.

"I'm so silly!" she cried. "My aunt sent me a box of lovely treats to eat! I'll go back to my room and get it!"

Sara went to fetch Becky and they pretended that they were decorating a huge banquet hall. When Ermengarde returned, they spread all the wonderful things to eat on a shawl that served as a tablecloth.

Suddenly, Miss Minchin burst into the room, white with anger. She hit Becky, and shouted at her.

"Go to your room immediately!"

She made Ermengarde take the treats away, and told Sara she would have no food the next day. Sara gazed at her, saying nothing, and this angered Miss Minchin.

"What are you thinking?" she demanded.

"I was wondering," Sara answered, "what my papa would say if he knew where I am tonight."

"You insolent child!" Miss Minchin shouted, shaking her violently. "Go to bed this instant!" As Sara went sadly to bed, a head peered in unnoticed through the skylight.

A Perfect Surprise

Sara lay down to sleep, imagining she had soft downy pillows and fleecy blankets. When she was woken a little while later by a sound, she felt too warm and snug to open her eyes. She was having a delightful dream that she was covered with a satin quilt and she didn't want to wake up. When at last she did open her eyes, she couldn't believe them.

"I am still dreaming!" she whispered. She *was* covered by a satin quilt. A fire was burning in the grate, a little kettle hissed on the hob, and a thick, warm rug lay on the floor. There were blankets and a little folding chair and table. On the table a wonderful meal was spread out, with a teapot ready to be filled. She touched everything and it was real. There was even a note that read "To the little girl in the attic. From a friend".

Sara rushed to Becky's room and dragged her over to see the wonderful changes. They had a feast of soup, sandwiches, muffins, toast, and tea, and it was all real.

"Do you think it could melt away, Miss?" Becky asked, cramming a sandwich into her mouth, just in case. At last, warm and fed, they shared the blankets between them and both went back to bed.

"If it ain't here in the morning," Becky said as she went off to her own room, "at least it was here tonight. And I'll never forget it!"

The Surprise Continues

But everything was still there in the morning. And, as the days passed, more and more wonderful things appeared while Sara was out or sleeping. Delicious, hot food—enough for her and Becky—arrived every morning and night.

The weather got worse and worse, and the cook sent Sara on more errands outside. Lavinia sneered at Sara's clothes, which got shabbier and shabbier. But Sara remained cheerful, happy in the knowledge that she had a secret friend watching out for her somewhere.

Miss Minchin had expected Sara and Becky to be miserable after she had told them off for eating Ermengarde's food, and she was puzzled that they were both increasingly cheerful. They even seemed to look better fed and healthier, though they were given so little food it should not have been possible. Miss Minchin took this as an insult.

"Sara Crewe looks well," she said to Miss Amelia. She was becoming suspicious—how could Sara look so healthy on such ill treatment?

A few days later, Sara went to answer a knock on the door. A man handed over a pile of parcels all addressed to "The little girl in the right-hand attic". As Miss Minchin was passing, she told Sara to take the parcels directly to the girl they were for.

"They are for me," Sara said. Miss Minchin looked at the label in confusion and told Sara to open the parcels.

The parcels were filled with pretty, comfortable clothes, including shoes, stockings, and a warm coat. There was a note pinned to them which read, "To be worn every day. Will be replaced when necessary".

Miss Minchin was disturbed and worried. Could she, she wondered, have been wrong about Sara? Perhaps the girl had some unknown rich relative. A rich relative would not like the way Sara was now being treated.

"Well," Miss Minchin said, "you had better go and put them on. No need for any more errands today."

When Sara walked into the schoolroom half an hour later, the other pupils were struck dumb. They were even more surprised when Miss Minchin told Sara to sit in her old place.

"Perhaps the diamond mines have appeared again," said Lavinia, bitterly.

That night, Sara had an idea. Among the things that had appeared in her room was a writing set. So she wrote a thank you note to the kind friend who was leaving her presents and left it with the tea things.

The next evening, the note was gone. But something else appeared. Sara and Becky heard a scratching at the skylight—it was the monkey again. Sara let him in. It was far too cold for the monkey to be outside, but too late to take him home.

"I shall let him sleep with me tonight, and take him back to the Indian gentleman tomorrow," Sara said.

Returning the Monkey

The next day, the Large Family were at Mr. Carrisford's house awaiting the return of Mr. Carmichael from Moscow. He brought bad news.

"She is not the child we are looking for," he said. "The girl I found is much younger than Captain Crewe's daughter."

"The search must start again!" Mr. Carrisford said.

"She must be somewhere," said Mr. Carmichael. "Let us give up on Paris. Let us start in London."

"There are lots of schools in London," Mr. Carrisford said. "There is a sad little girl in the one next door. She is as unlike the Crewe girl as any child could be."

At that moment, Ram Dass came in to say that the little girl from next door had just arrived.

"Your monkey ran away again," Sara said, stepping into the room. "Shall I give him to the lascar?"

"How do you know he is a lascar?" asked Mr. Carrisford, astonished.

"Oh, I know what lascars are," Sara explained to him. "I was born in India."

Mr. Carrisford sat up suddenly, with a strange expression on his face. Sara told him that she had been brought to Miss Minchin's as a pupil, but when her father died she had been left a beggar.

"How did your father lose his money?" he asked.

"He had a friend he trusted too much," Sara replied. "His friend took his money for the diamond mines."

Mr. Carrisford could not believe his ears.

"What was your father's name?" he asked. "Tell me."

"Ralph Crewe," Sara answered.

"It is the child—the child!" he cried. The whole story came tumbling out. Sara learned that Mr. Carrisford had not cheated her papa at all, but had genuinely thought he had lost all the money. He had fallen ill with fever, and by the time he recovered, Captain Crewe was dead. Mr. Carrisford had been searching for Sara ever since.

"And, all the while, I was just the other side of the wall," whispered Sara.

At that moment, Miss Minchin came in. She had seen Sara go into the house and had followed her to apologize for the disturbance.

"She is not going back with you," Mr. Carrisford said sternly.

Mr. Carmichael explained everything to Miss Minchin, who felt it was the worst thing that had ever happened to her. When she heard that Sara was, after all, to inherit a huge fortune from the diamond mines, she made one last attempt to win her back.

"Her father left her in my care," she said. "If it weren't for me, she would have starved in the street."

"She would have been better off in the street than starving in your attic!" Mr. Carrisford said. "Sara, how would you like to live here with me from now on?"

Of course, Sara gratefully accepted Mr. Carrisford's offer. Miss Minchin stormed home to find Miss Amelia. But Miss Amelia turned on her.

"I am always afraid to say things to you for fear of making you angry," she said, "but you should have been less severe on Sara Crewe. She was a good child, and too clever for you. She saw that you were hard-hearted and that I was a fool. And all the time she behaved like a little princess!"

That evening the other girls in the school found out what was going on. Ermengarde brought in a letter from Sara that explained everything. "There were diamond mines!" she said.

When Becky went up to her attic room that night, Ram Dass was waiting for her with a letter. She was to move to Mr. Carrisford's house and live with Sara.

Sara did not forget what it felt like to be poor. The next day, she asked to go to the shop where she had once bought six buns. The woman in the shop remembered Sara giving away five of her buns to a hungry little girl. Sara said that she would like to pay for bread and buns for all the poor children who came to the shop from then onward.

"Do you know where the little girl is now?" Sara asked.

"Why, she is here! She works for me," the woman said.

"Then let her be the one to give bread and buns to the poor children!" Sara said. And as she and Mr. Carrisford rode away in the carriage, Sara felt happy.

THE END

The Secret Garden

Mary Lennox was a skinny, plain little girl who always wore a sour look. Her hair was thin and yellow, and her face was rather yellow, too, because she was always ill and stayed indoors. Mary lived in India with her mother and father, but her father was always busy and her mother had never really wanted her. She was looked after by servants. Everyone did whatever Mary wanted, and she became very selfish and spoiled.

One hot morning, when Mary was nine years old, her own servant, Saidie, didn't come to dress her as usual. Mary had a tantrum, but no one would tell her what was going on.

When she was tired of being cross, Mary wandered outside and made a pretend garden by sticking red flowers into the earth. She overheard her mother talking with a young army officer. Her mother was beautiful and wore pretty lace dresses and Mary loved looking at her. But this morning her mother looked scared.

"Is it so very bad?" Mary heard her say to the officer.

"Awful," he answered.

Mary listened as the officer explained that a disease called cholera had broken out.

Just then, a terrible wail came from the servants' quarters, and Mary's mother clutched the man's arm.

"I am afraid someone has died," whispered the officer.

Mary soon learned that it was her servant, Saidie, who had fallen ill in the night. Awful things happened quickly after that and more servants died.

Mary hid in her nursery all of the next day, but no one came to look for her. It seemed she was entirely forgotten. The house grew quiet and Mary slept for a long time.

When she woke, a man she had never seen before opened the door. He was horrified to see her, but Mary was only cross.

"I am Mary Lennox. I fell asleep when everyone had the cholera. Why was I forgotten?" she said, stamping her foot.

"Poor little thing!" he said. "There's nobody left."

And so Mary discovered that both her father and mother had died. Mary didn't know her parents well enough to miss them, and she was far too selfish to be sad about it.

Mary lived with a vicar's family until she could be sent back to England. The vicar had five children, who argued all the time. Mary didn't like them. On her second day, she was making another garden when one of the boys suggested she plant some flowers in amongst the rocks. Mary shouted at him and he began to tease her.

"Mistress Mary, quite contrary! How does your garden grow?" he sang.

Soon all the children called her "Mistress Mary" and Mary hated it. She was relieved when the news came that she was to move to England and live with her uncle, Mr. Archibald Craven, at Misselthwaite Manor.

Misselthwaite Manor

Mary traveled by ship to England. It was a long and difficult journey. The officer's wife who had been asked to look after Mary on the ship was glad to hand her over to Mr. Craven's housekeeper in London.

Mrs. Medlock, the housekeeper, was plump with red cheeks and black beady eyes. Mary thought she looked unpleasant. Mrs. Medlock thought Mary looked spoiled.

They took a long train journey. Mary sat silently until, eventually, Mrs. Medlock said, "You're going to a strange place, lass. It's a big, gloomy house that's six hundred years old and has nearly a hundred rooms. It's right on the edge of the moor. Mr. Craven won't take any notice of you. He sees no one. He has a crooked back, and that set him off on the wrong foot. Until he married he was a bitter, miserable young man. His wife was a sweet, pretty young thing and changed him. But now she's dead, he doesn't care about anybody."

Mary was not concerned. She sat crossly while the rain poured down the windowpanes. She soon fell asleep and, when the train stopped, Mrs. Medlock shook her awake. A carriage took them across the moor to Misselthwaite. Mary looked out of the window, curious, at last, to see where they were going. She felt the long drive would never end.

"I don't like this place at all," she grumbled.

Finally, they stopped in front of a long, low house built around a stone courtyard.

Mrs. Medlock led Mary through a maze of staircases and corridors to her room. There was a fire in the grate and a meal on the table.

"Well, here you are! This room and the one next door are yours," Mrs. Medlock said. "You are to stay in them. Don't you forget that!"

In the morning, Mary opened her eyes to see a young housemaid cleaning the fireplace. The housemaid was named Martha. She saw Mary looking out of the window at the expanse of dull, purplish land that stretched into the distance.

"That's the moor," said Martha. "Do you like it?"

"No," said Mary. "I hate it. Who is going to dress me?"

"Can't you dress yourself?" Martha asked.

"No," replied Mary. "My servants always dressed me."

"Well, it's time you learned," said Martha. But, just this time, Martha did help Mary put on the new clothes that Mr. Craven had told Mrs. Medlock to buy. They were much nicer than the clothes she had worn to travel back from India.

At first, Mary ignored Martha as she chatted. In India, she had grown up in a house where servants were ignored, and she wasn't interested in what a maid had to say. But Mary soon began to listen as Martha talked about her home, her eleven brothers and sisters, and how they all played on the moor. She especially liked to hear about Dickon, who had a pony of his own that he had found on the moor. But Mary did not admit this.

A Mystery

The next day, at breakfast, Mary did not feel like eating her porridge. Martha hated to see food wasted.

"My brothers and sisters have never had full stomachs in their lives. They're as hungry as young hawks," she said.

"I don't know what it is to be hungry," said Mary.

"Well, it would do you good to try it," Martha said. "Put on your coat and go and play outside."

"I don't want to," said Mary.

"Go on, now," Martha said. "Our Dickon goes off on the moor by himself for hours."

As there was nothing else to do, Mary did go outside after all. Before she went, Martha told her a story about a garden that no one had been in for ten years.

"Mr. Craven shut it when his wife died. It was her garden. He locked the door and buried the key," Martha said.

As Mary walked, she thought about the garden. She wondered whether she would be able to find it. She followed paths and walked through walled gardens until she saw an old man digging.

"What's through that door?" Mary asked him.

"A kitchen garden," he answered. "There are more beyond this one and an orchard, too."

Once in the orchard, Mary could see treetops peeping over a wall, and a bird with a bright red breast perched in one of them. The wall carried on past the orchard and Mary wondered if it was the wall of the secret garden.

Mary thought about the key to the garden. Why had Mr. Craven buried it? If he loved his wife so much, why did he hate her garden? For a long time she looked for a door, but couldn't find one. At last she walked back to the gardener and told him about the pretty bird she'd seen.

The man whistled, and the bird landed near his foot.

"What kind of a bird is he?" Mary asked.

"He's a robin redbreast. Are you the lass from India?"

"Yes," Mary nodded. "What is your name?"

"Ben Weatherstaff," he answered with a rough chuckle, "and this little bird is the only friend I've got."

"I have no friends at all," said Mary.

"You're a good bit like me, then," Ben said. "Neither of us is very pretty and we're both as sour as we look."

Suddenly a clear, bright sound filled the air. The robin had flown to a tree near Mary and burst into cheerful song.

"He wants to be friends with you!" Ben said.

"Would you be friends with me?" Mary asked the robin.

"You sound like Dickon talking to his wild creatures."

"I've heard all about Dickon," said Mary.

The robin shook his wings and flew away over the wall.

"He's flown into the garden with no door!" Mary cried.

"He lives there," said Ben. "Among the old rose trees."

"I should like to see the rose trees," said Mary. "There must be a door somewhere."

"None as anyone can find. Don't poke your nose in where it's not wanted. Now run along," Ben snapped.

The Garden Without a Door

Every day seemed the same to Mary. Each morning she ate a little breakfast, and then realized that if she didn't go out she'd have to stay in and do nothing—so she went out. Little did she know, this was the best thing she could have done. The fresh air was good for her and it soon put color in her cheeks and a sparkle in her eye. After a few days, she was hungry enough to eat all of her breakfast, and that pleased Martha.

Mary still hoped to find the door to the deserted garden. One day, she was looking up at a spray of ivy hanging down from the wall when she saw the robin again. He twittered and hopped along, and Mary ran after him. Poor, thin, plain Mary actually looked pretty as she played. At last the robin flew to the top of a tree on the other side of the wall.

"He lives in the garden without a door," Mary said to herself. "How I wish I could see what it's like!"

The hidden garden gave her something to think about. At last, she felt pleased to have come to Misselthwaite. In India, she had always been too hot and never cared about anything. Now, she stayed outdoors all day, and when she sat down for her supper she felt hungry and well. She was no longer cross when Martha chattered away, and even quite liked to hear her talk.

A Cry in the Wind

One evening, Mary asked Martha why Mr. Craven hated the garden.

"There was an old tree with a branch like a seat," said Martha. "Mrs. Craven used to sit there. But, one day, the branch broke and she fell and died. The doctors thought Mr. Craven might go out of his mind."

Mary looked into the fire and listened to the wind. But she began to hear something else.

"Do you hear anyone crying?" she asked Martha.

"No," Martha answered. "It's the wind. Sometimes it sounds as if someone is lost on the moor, wailing."

"But listen," said Mary. "It sounds like it's coming from the house."

"It's the wind," Martha repeated firmly.

The next day it poured rain, and Mary couldn't go out. She wandered around the house, exploring rooms she had never been in. On her way back to her own floor, she heard the crying again.

Mary put her hand on a tapestry next to her and, to her surprise, a door hidden behind it fell open. Mary peered through the door and saw Mrs. Medlock marching angrily along a corridor toward her.

"I heard crying," said Mary.

"You did not hear crying," Mrs. Medlock said, and she grabbed Mary and dragged her back to her room.

Mary sat on the rug, trembling with rage.

"There *was* someone crying!" she said to herself.

The Buried Key

Two days later, the sky was a startling blue and Mary could go outside again. Spring was coming. She looked at the green spikes of crocuses and daffodils coming up through the grass, and then she saw the robin pecking in a pile of freshly dug earth. There was something partly buried in the earth that looked like a ring. The robin flew away and Mary stooped to take a look. She brushed away the soil. It was a large key!

"Perhaps it's been buried for ten years," she whispered. "Perhaps it's the key to the garden!"

Mary looked at the key for a long time. She was curious and desperately wanted to see what was inside the garden and what had happened to the old rose trees. She put the key in her pocket, so that if she *did* ever find the hidden door she would be ready.

While Mary was outdoors, Martha went to visit her mother. When she got back, she said she had shared news of Mary with her mother, brothers, and sisters. They were all eager to hear more and Mary promised to tell Martha new stories about India. Martha gave Mary a present from her mother.

"What is it?" Mary asked in wonder.

"It's a skipping rope!" cried Martha. "So, you have elephants and tigers and camels in India, but no skipping ropes?"

Martha had to show Mary what to do, but she skipped until her cheeks were red.

Mary's Garden

As she skipped in the garden, Mary felt the heavy key in her pocket. When she saw the robin, she said, "Robin, yesterday you showed me the key. Now show me the door!"

What happened next seemed like magic. No sooner had she finished speaking than a gust of wind blew the hanging ivy aside and, for just a moment, Mary glimpsed a doorknob. She quickly pushed the ivy away, and there, right in front of her eyes, was the hidden door! She took the key from her pocket and turned it in the lock. The old door creaked as Mary pushed it slowly open and she took a few cautious steps forward. At last she had found it! At last she was standing inside the secret garden.

A thick tangle of climbing roses covered the high walls, but only their leafless stems remained. The roses had grown over the other trees, and hung in curtains and made bridges between them. Mary wondered if they were dead—she didn't know enough about plants to tell. But the pale green spikes of growing plants pushed through the grass, so Mary knew that the garden was not completely dead. The grass under her feet was so thick that there didn't seem to be room for the shoots to grow. Mary dug away the weeds and grass around the new spikes with a piece of wood. She worked carefully and for a long time, until it was time to go in for lunch.

At the manor, Martha served Mary a lunch of meat and rice pudding, which Mary ate hungrily.

"I wish I had a little spade," Mary said to Martha after she had eaten. "Then I could dig and make a garden of my own."

There was a shop in the village that sold garden sets and seeds. Martha suggested Mary should write to Dickon and ask him to buy them and bring them over. Mary had enough money, as Mr. Craven left some for her each week. She was excited about getting a new spade, but even more excited that she might meet Dickon.

The sun shone for a week, and every day Mary went back to work in the secret garden, digging and pulling up weeds with her hands and a piece of wood. Then, one day, on her way to the garden, she saw a boy standing under a tree playing a wooden pipe. He was about twelve years old and had a turned-up nose and rosy red cheeks. A squirrel clung to the trunk of the tree, and two rabbits sat nearby. She knew at once it had to be Dickon!

Dickon had brought the tools and some seeds for Mary, and offered to plant them. But, when Dickon asked where her garden was, Mary didn't know what to say.

"Can you keep a secret?" she said, clutching at his sleeve. "I've stolen a garden. Nobody wants it, or cares for it though. And no one ever goes there."

Meeting Mr. Craven

"Where is this garden?" asked Dickon.

Mary took him to the door, lifted the hanging ivy, and led him into the secret garden. For two or three minutes, Dickon just stood and stared.

"I never thought I'd see this place," he said at last.

"Did you know about it?" asked Mary.

Dickon nodded. Mary asked Dickon if he thought the roses were all dead, but he cut a stem open to show her that they were still alive inside. Dickon saw the patches Mary had cleared around the bulbs.

"There's a lot of work to do here!" he said.

"Will you come again and help me to do it?" asked Mary. "Oh, do come, Dickon!"

"I'll come every day if you want me to," he answered.

They worked happily together, until the big clock struck the hour for lunch and Mary had to go inside.

Mary ate lunch quickly, eager to get back to Dickon, but then Martha said Mr. Craven had returned from London and wanted to see her. Mrs. Medlock led her to a room she had never seen before. Mr. Craven was sitting in an armchair by the fire. He had high, crooked shoulders and looked awkwardly at Mary.

"Are you well, child? Is there anything you want?" he asked.

"Might I have a bit of earth to plant seeds?"

"You can have as much earth as you want," he sighed. "Take it and make things grow. Now please go, as I am tired."

Finding Colin

That night, Mary was woken by wind and rain beating against her window. She lay and listened and soon realized it wasn't just the wind she could hear—she could hear the crying sound again, too. Mary took a candle and padded to the corridor she had found behind the tapestry. The crying led her into a big room, where a boy lay sobbing in bed. Mary crept toward him.

"Are you a ghost?" he sniffled when he saw Mary.

"No," she answered. "Are you?"

"No, I am Colin Craven. Who are you?"

"I am Mary Lennox. Mr. Craven is my uncle."

"He's my father," said the boy.

"Your father!" Mary gasped. "He has a child!"

Colin explained that he hated to be looked at, and that he was always ill.

"If I live, I may grow lumps on my back and be a hunchback, but I shan't live," he said. "My mother died soon after I was born and I make my father miserable."

"He hates the garden because she died," Mary said to herself.

"What garden?" Colin asked.

"Oh, just…just a garden she used to like," Mary stammered. She quickly changed the subject and told Colin all about her voyage from India. Colin told Mary how everyone had to do as he said, as being ill made him angry.

"How old are you?" Colin asked her.

"I'm ten," she answered, "and so are you, because when you were born the garden door was locked and the key was buried. And it has been locked for ten years."

"What garden door was locked? Where was the key buried? Who buried it?" asked Colin.

"Mr. Craven," said Mary, nervously. "He locked the door and buried the key. But I found it."

Colin kept asking questions.

"I'll make the servants take me to the garden!" he said.

"Don't do that!" Mary cried. "If you don't tell anyone I promise I'll find a way for us to go there together."

Once Colin agreed to her plan, Mary relaxed a little.

Martha was alarmed when Mary told her that she had found Colin, and then astonished that Colin had been willing to talk to her. Soon afterward, Colin even sent for Mary. Mary told him all about Dickon—how he was a friend of the animals and how they trusted him. When Colin started to talk about dying, Mary insisted that they talk about other things.

The two children soon realized that they were cousins and were laughing when Colin's doctor and Mrs. Medlock suddenly walked in. The doctor was worried that Mary made Colin too excited. But Colin said that Mary made him feel better and he would continue to see her. The doctor agreed, but warned Colin not to forget that he was very ill.

An Argument

For a whole week after that it rained, and Mary spent hours every day talking to Colin. But, on the first morning when the sky was blue again, she ran straight to the secret garden. Dickon was already digging and working hard when she arrived. Mary was thrilled to meet his fox cub, Captain, and a rook called Soot. She was excited, too, to tell him about Colin.

"If he was out here with us, he wouldn't be watching and waiting for lumps to grow on his back, and he'd be healthier," said Dickon. "It'd be good for him."

But, when Mary went to see Colin later on, he was furious with her.

"Why didn't you come to see me earlier?" he demanded.

"I was working in the garden with Dickon," answered Mary.

"I won't let that boy come here if you spend time with him instead of me!" he said.

"If you send Dickon away, I'll never come to visit you again," Mary shouted. "You're so selfish!"

"I'm not as selfish as you," snapped Colin, "because I'm always ill, and I'm sure there is a lump coming on my back, and I'm going to die."

"You're not going to die!" shouted Mary. "You just want people to feel sorry for you."

"Get out of my room!" shouted Colin, in a rage.

"I'm going," cried Mary. "And I won't come back!"

Animals in the Bedroom

That night, Mary was woken by terrible screaming and crying. She put her hands over her ears.

"Somebody ought to make him stop!" she shouted.

But just then, the nurse rushed in and begged her to go to Colin's room. Mary ran along the corridor.

"Just stop!" she shouted at Colin. "I hate you! Everybody hates you!"

"I can't stop!" he gasped.

"Yes, you can!" shouted Mary. "All that's wrong with you is a terrible temper!"

"I felt the lump," cried Colin. "I shall have a hunch on my back and I shall die."

"You didn't feel a lump!" Mary snapped. "There's nothing at all the matter with your back. Let me see!"

Mary looked at his spine and ran her hand down it.

"There's not a single lump there except for your backbones!" she said.

Colin breathed a sigh of relief. No one had ever spoken so crossly to him before, but neither had anyone ever reassured him like that.

"Do you think I'll grow up?" he asked his nurse.

"You probably will," she answered, "if you do not get into such a temper, do as you are told, and go out into the fresh air as much as you can."

"I would like to go there with you, Mary," said Colin, at last, "if Dickon will come and push my chair. I do so want to see Dickon and the fox and the rook."

The next day, Mary and Dickon made a plan. Mary ran to Colin's room while Dickon waited.

"It's so beautiful outside!" Mary said. "Spring has arrived! There are buds everywhere." She threw open the window to let in the fresh air and told Colin that Dickon was coming to visit him with his animals.

Colin couldn't wait to meet Dickon and the animals and told his nurse to bring them straight to his room.

"A boy, and a fox, and a crow, and two squirrels, and a newborn lamb are coming to see me this morning. I want them brought upstairs," he said.

The nurse gave a gasp and covered it up with a cough. "Yes, sir," she answered.

"I'll tell you what you can do," added Colin, waving his hand. "You can tell Martha to bring them here. The boy is Martha's brother. His name is Dickon!"

Dickon came in smiling with the newborn lamb in his arms, the fox cub trotting by his side, a crow on his shoulder, and two squirrels. Colin couldn't believe his eyes. Dickon put the lamb on Colin's lap, pulled a bottle from his pocket, and fed the lamb while answering all of Colin's questions. The three of them looked at pictures of flowers in a book that Mr. Craven had sent to Mary.

"I'm going to see all these flowers!" cried Colin, and together they planned a visit to the garden.

The Secret Uncovered

It wasn't long before Dickon pushed Colin's wheelchair to the ivy-covered walls around the secret garden.

"I used to walk here and think about finding the garden," said Mary. "And that is where I found the key. And here is the door! Dickon, push him in quickly!"

Little green leaves had crept over the walls and trees, and the grass was splashed with the gold and purple of crocuses. As the warm sun shone on Colin's face, he cried out, "I shall get well! And I shall live forever and ever!"

Colin watched as Mary and Dickon worked in the garden. They brought him things to look at: buds, a woodpecker's feather, the empty shell of a newly hatched bird. The afternoon was packed with new things, and the sun shone golden and warm on them.

"I never want this afternoon to end," Colin said, "but I'll come back tomorrow, and the day after. I will see everything grow here, and I'll grow here myself!"

But suddenly Colin stopped.

"Who's that man?" he whispered in alarm.

Mary and Dickon looked around to see Ben Weatherstaff glaring over the wall at them from a ladder. He shook his fist at Mary and shouted at her.

"You young bad 'un. You had no business poking around here!"

But he stopped quickly when he saw Dickon pushing the wheelchair behind her.

"Do you know who I am?" demanded Colin.

Ben Weatherstaff was stunned.

"Aye, I do—you are the poor cripple," he said.

"I am not a cripple!" Colin cried out, furiously.

"Don't you have a crooked back?"

"No!" shouted Colin.

Then, as Dickon held his arm, Colin slowly put his feet onto the grass and moved his weight onto his thin legs. For the first time, he stood upright.

Tears ran down Ben Weatherstaff's cheeks.

"Eh!" he said. "The lies folk tell! You'll be a man yet!"

"Get down from the ladder, and Mary will let you in," Colin said. "I want to talk to you."

So Mary opened the door and let Ben inside.

"Please keep our secret," said Colin. "I want to visit the garden as much as I can."

Ben admitted that for years he had come into the secret garden and pruned the roses, because he had been so fond of Colin's mother. But now he was too old to climb over the wall.

"How'd you like to plant a rose? I can get you a rose in a pot," said Ben.

"Go and get it!" said Colin, excitedly. Dickon took his spade and helped Colin to dig the hole. Ben brought the rose from the greenhouse.

"Here, lad," he said. "Set it in the earth."

"It's planted!" said Colin, at last, and he looked up at the sky, glowing with happiness.

Dickon's Mother

One evening, Dickon told his mother all about Colin and the secret garden.

"My word!" she said. "It was a good thing that little lass came to the manor. It's been the making of her and it's saved him. What do the folk at the manor make of it all?"

"They don't know," answered Dickon. "Colin has to keep complaining and pretending that he is still unwell, so that they don't guess. If the doctor knew that Colin was recovering, he'd write and tell Mr. Craven, and Colin wants to show his father himself."

Day by day, Colin had begun to eat more. He put on weight and his cheeks gained a healthy glow. One day, Dickon stood on the grass and slowly went through some simple muscle exercises. Colin watched them with widening eyes.

"You must do them gently at first and be careful not to tire yourself. Rest in between times and take deep breaths and don't do too much," said Dickon.

"I'll be careful," said Colin. "Can you show me, please, Dickon?"

Colin could do the exercises while he was sitting down but, after a while, he gently did a few standing on his newly steady feet. Mary began to do them, too.

The secret garden grew more beautiful each day, with flowers in every tiny space.

One morning, Colin was weeding when he stood up and stretched.

"Mary! Dickon!" he called. "Just look at me! I'm well! I shall live forever and ever! I shall find out about people and creatures and everything that grows, just like Dickon. I feel as if I want to shout out something thankful and joyful!"

Just then, the door in the ivy-covered wall opened, and a woman walked in.

"It's Mother!" Dickon cried. "I told her where the door to the secret garden was hidden."

Colin had heard a lot about Mrs. Sowerby, and was delighted that she had come.

"Are you surprised because I am so well?" he asked. She put her hand on his shoulder and wiped the tears away from her eyes.

"Yes, I am," she said. "I knew your mother and you look so much like her that it made my heart jump!"

"Do you think," said Colin, a little awkwardly, "that it will make my father like me?"

"Oh, yes, dear lad," she answered, smiling kindly. They led her around the garden and told her everything they had been doing. Mrs. Sowerby had brought them a picnic, and she sat and watched as they ate it. She was fun and made them laugh. Then they told her how difficult it was to keep pretending that Colin was ill.

"You won't have to keep it up much longer," she said. "Mr. Craven is sure to come home soon."

A Surprise Visit

While the secret garden was coming alive, Archibald Craven was traveling around Europe. He was never happy but, one morning, a feeling of calm crept over him. He had been miserable for ten years, but now he thought of home. He wondered about his son, but was afraid of what he would find if he went back. As the summer passed, he felt stronger—just as Colin did playing outside in the fresh air. Then, one day, he dreamed he heard his wife calling him into the garden. When he woke, there was a letter from Mrs. Sowerby waiting for him. She reminded him that they had met once before on the moor, and that they had spoken about Mary. She said she thought there was now good reason for him to return home.

"I will go back to Misselthwaite at once," he said.

On his journey, he thought about Colin, and wondered whether the boy was dying. In just a few days, he was home. On the drive across the moor to the house he decided to find the buried key to the garden. He had been thinking about all the happy times they had spent there, and wanted to see it again. But, when he arrived at the manor, Mrs. Medlock told him that Colin was already in the garden. Shocked, Mr. Craven walked to where the thick ivy hung over the door, and heard laughter coming from inside the walls. He heard running feet, and then the door was flung open and a boy ran straight into him.

He was a tall, handsome boy, glowing with life and, when he threw the thick hair back from his forehead, his gray eyes made Mr. Craven gasp. "Who...What?" he stammered.

This was not the meeting Colin had planned, but he drew himself up to his very tallest.

"Father," he said, "I'm Colin. You can't believe it, can you? It was the garden that did it, and Mary and Dickon and the animals. We kept it a secret!"

Mr. Craven put his hands on the boy's shoulders and held him still. He dared not speak for a moment.

"Take me into the garden, my boy," he said at last. "And tell me all about it."

The garden was filled with autumn color. Late roses climbed in the sunshine. Mr. Craven looked around him in wonder. They sat down under a tree, all except Colin, who wanted to stand while he told the story.

"So now the garden doesn't need to be a secret any more," Colin said, at last. "And I'm never going to use the wheelchair again."

Ben Weatherstaff had been listening and dashed back to the house to tell the servants what had happened. Mrs. Medlock shrieked with delight when they saw the master of Misselthwaite coming across the lawn, looking happier than they had ever seen him. And, by his side, with his head up in the air, walking strongly and steadily, was Master Colin.

THE END

Heidi

One bright sunny summer morning, a five-year-old girl climbed the winding path leading up to the Alm mountain in Switzerland. Her name was Heidi, and her parents had died when she was a baby. Since then she had been looked after by her Aunt Dete, who now walked beside her. On the way up, Dete's friend Barbel came out to say hello. "Where are you taking Heidi?" she asked.

"Up to her grandfather's," Dete replied.

"The old man everyone calls the Alm-Uncle?" Barbel exclaimed. "He'll never be able to look after her!"

"I have no choice," Dete said sadly. "I have a new job in Frankfurt, and I can't take Heidi with me."

"But the Alm-Uncle is almost a hermit—we never see him in the village or at church," said Barbel. "All he has are his two goats. How will he provide for her?"

"He's Heidi's grandfather. She will be fine with him," Dete insisted. She looked around. "Now, where is she?"

"There, I see her!" cried Barbel. "She is with Peter, the boy who looks after the goats."

A short distance away, Heidi was walking with a boy a few years older than she was. The two children were barefoot, chatting happily and laughing together while a herd of goats scampered nearby. Dete smiled as she watched them. "I think Heidi will feel right at home here," she told Barbel, sounding very relieved indeed.

Heidi's grandfather was a gruff old man. He was not pleased when Dete left the young girl with him.

But Heidi was enchanted with her new surroundings. She gazed at the pine trees and listened to the wind singing as it moved through the branches.

Grandfather picked up the bundle of Heidi's clothes that Aunt Dete had left. "We'd better put these away inside," he said. "Don't you want to put your shoes on?"

"No, I want to go about like the goats!" Heidi replied.

For the first time in years, Grandfather smiled. "So you shall," he said.

Grandfather's house was just one room, with his bed in the corner. Heidi wondered where she would sleep.

"Sleep wherever you wish," said Grandfather.

There was a ladder that led up to the hayloft, and Heidi climbed it. When she discovered all the soft, sweet-smelling hay, she cried out with delight. "I'll sleep up here!" she said.

Grandfather brought up a sheet to put over the hay, as well as a blanket to keep Heidi warm.

At supper time, Grandfather made a simple meal of bread and cheese. He ladled some fresh, creamy goat's milk into a mug for Heidi and she drank it eagerly.

"I have never tasted such delicious milk!" she declared.

That night, as she snuggled into her bed, Heidi could see the moon shining down through the little window of the hayloft. She fell asleep to the sound of the wind whistling through the pines, a sweet smile on her face.

In the Pasture

A shrill whistle woke Heidi the next morning. She opened her eyes to the bright sunlight streaming in through her little window. Excited, she jumped out of bed, dressed quickly and ran outside.

Peter, the goatherd she had met the day before, was waiting for Grandfather to bring his goats out to join the herd.

"Would you like to go to the pasture with Peter and the goats?" Grandfather asked Heidi.

"Oh, yes, please!" said Heidi enthusiastically.

Grandfather packed them some food and milk. Then Peter, Heidi, and the goats set off up the Alm.

All morning, Heidi scampered among the brightly colored wild flowers and played with the goats. Little Swan and Little Bear, who belonged to Grandfather, were Heidi's favorites.

Peter showed her where an eagle had its nest on a rocky cliff, and they watched it soar into the air. Heidi spotted snowfields higher up the mountain, icy white against the deep blue sky. She was amazed by all she saw.

At midday, they sat under a pine tree and ate the lunch Grandfather had packed. Heidi drank all her milk very quickly, so Peter got her some more, straight from Little Swan. It was warm and sweet and delicious.

Late in the afternoon, when the sunset turned the sky to fire, Heidi and Peter made their way back down from the pasture. Heidi had never been happier.

Peter's Grandmother

Heidi went to the pasture with Peter and the goats every day that summer. She and Peter became good friends and Heidi grew strong and healthy in the fresh mountain air.

When autumn winds began to blow, Heidi went up the mountain less and less. When winter arrived, and snow covered the Alm, Peter went to school down in the village of Dörfli. He told Heidi that his grandmother found the winter days lonely and that Heidi should visit.

Heidi pestered her reluctant grandfather until eventually he bundled her into blankets, set her on his old wooden sled, and took her to Peter's cottage. Anxious to avoid Peter's family, he left Heidi at the door.

Peter's mother welcomed Heidi and showed her to Peter's grandmother, who sat at a spinning wheel. On hearing that the old lady was blind, Heidi was very upset at the thought she could no longer see the beautiful snowy mountains. So, she held her hand and described the scene from the cottage window as best she could.

"Tell me about your grandfather, Heidi," said Peter's grandmother. "I knew him when we were younger."

Heidi talked fondly of Grandfather, how he could make anything out of wood and how much she had enjoyed the summer in Alm. The old lady listened intently, surprised at how happy the little girl seemed.

Heidi came to visit often that winter, brightening the old woman's days.

Visitors

The years passed quickly and happily for Heidi, and by the time she was eight years old she had learned many things from her grandfather.

One spring morning the pastor from Dörfli came to see Grandfather.

"Heidi needs an education," the pastor said. "Move down to the village next winter so she can go to school with the other children. It will be good for you to live among your neighbors again." Grandfather refused.

"Heidi does not need to go to school," he said. "She is happy here and doesn't need other children." Shaking his head at the old man's stubbornness, the pastor left. The very next day, Aunt Dete came to see them.

"I am taking Heidi back to Frankfurt with me," she told Grandfather. Dete then explained that she knew of a young girl who could not walk and spent her days in a wheelchair. Her father was looking for a bright little girl to be her companion and Heidi would be perfect.

Heidi was distraught and refused to leave. Her Grandfather did not want her to leave either, but Dete insisted she would enjoy Frankfurt.

"Take her, then," snapped Grandfather angrily, "and don't ever come back!"

Dete and Heidi left in a rush. Heidi wanted to say goodbye to everyone, but Dete said there was no time.

"You can bring them presents from Frankfurt," she said. Convinced she would return soon, Heidi followed Dete.

A New Life for Heidi

Clara Sesemann sat in her wheelchair in the study of her house in Frankfurt, as she did every day. Her mother had died years ago, and her father was often away on business, so Clara was looked after by a strict woman called Miss Rottenmeier. Miss Rottenmeier sat calmly sewing, while Clara fidgeted and fretted. She had been waiting all day for Heidi to arrive.

"When will they get here?" she asked for the tenth time in an hour. At that moment the door opened, and a servant brought in Heidi and Aunt Dete.

"Hmmm," sniffed Miss Rottenmeier, studying Heidi through disapproving eyes. "She looks far too young. Clara is twelve years old, and we expected a companion of her own age. How old is Heidi?"

"Er…" Dete hesitated. "I'm not sure exactly…"

"I am eight years old," Heidi declared.

"And what books have you read?" Miss Rottenmeier asked, sounding somewhat scary.

"I haven't read any," Heidi replied. "I can't read yet."

Miss Rottenmeier was shocked and remained silent.

"You can have lessons with me, Heidi," Clara said gently. "The Professor is kind, but his lessons can be a bit boring. If we have them together, it will be fun." She smiled warmly. Heidi liked Clara but Miss Rottenmeier had been very unwelcoming and Heidi really wasn't sure she would like her new life.

The End of a Long Day

Aunt Dete left quickly, and Heidi stayed with Clara until it was time for dinner. A servant named Sebastian came to push Clara's wheelchair into the large and ornate dining room.

Heidi had never seen such fine plates or such a beautiful tablecloth. She was pleased to see a soft white bread roll next to her plate. Peter's grandmother loved this type of bread.

"I can take her one as a present," Heidi thought, slipping the roll into her pocket.

When Sebastian served Heidi some meat, she looked up at him and asked, "Is all that for me?"

Trying not to smile, Sebastian nodded.

"Heidi, mind your manners!" scolded Miss Rottenmeier. "I see you have a lot to learn! You must never speak to the servants."

Miss Rottenmeier continued telling Heidi the rules she was to follow: how to enter and leave a room, how to keep her things tidy, how to eat properly… Miss Rottenmeier droned on for so long that Heidi fell asleep in her chair. She was very tired indeed!

"Never in my life have I come across anything like this child!" Miss Rottenmeier shouted. Clara began to giggle, which made Miss Rottenmeier even angrier.

But not even the shouting and laughter woke Heidi, and she had to be carried to her room and put to bed. Her first day in Frankfurt was over.

When Heidi woke up the next morning, she did not remember where she was. Looking through the window, she could see no grass, and no pine trees—only tall buildings. This gave her a strange, sad feeling.

After breakfast, Clara's kind and patient teacher, the Professor, arrived. Miss Rottenmeier was eager to tell him how much Heidi had to learn.

"She cannot even read!" she said. "I am sure she will hold Clara back in her studies." But the Professor calmly assured her that he could teach both girls. He would start by teaching Heidi the alphabet. Miss Rottenmeier left in a huff.

Moments later there was a crash in the schoolroom, and Miss Rottenmeier rushed back in. A table lay on its side, school books were scattered, and a stream of black ink ran across the carpet. Heidi was nowhere to be seen.

"What has that troublesome child done now?" the furious Miss Rottenmeier demanded.

"It was an accident," Clara explained. "Heidi heard something in the street and ran so quickly to see what it was that she bumped into the table. It wasn't her fault."

Miss Rottenmeier found Heidi standing at the front door.

"I thought I heard the wind rushing through the pines," Heidi explained. "But I can't see any trees."

"Do you think we live in a forest, foolish girl?" Miss Rottenmeier snapped. "If this ever happens again you will be punished. Do you understand?"

"Yes," said Heidi. "I promise to sit still from now on."

The Church Tower

In the afternoon, when Clara was resting, Heidi sneaked out of the house, hoping to find a place where she could see the mountains she loved.

She met a friendly boy about her own age playing a barrel organ, and she asked him if he knew of such a place.

"You can try going to the top of the church tower," he suggested. "I'll show you if you like."

When they got to the church, Heidi knocked on the door. It was opened by a caretaker, who didn't believe that Heidi wanted to climb the tower. He was about to send her away, but her eyes were so full of longing that he changed his mind.

"Come with me," he said, leading her up a narrow, winding staircase. When they reached the top, the caretaker held Heidi up to the tiny window so she could look out.

Heidi couldn't see any mountains anywhere.

"It's not what I expected," she said sadly.

When they got downstairs, Heidi spotted a basket near the caretaker's room. In it was a large ginger cat with seven kittens nestled beside her.

"How sweet they are!" Heidi exclaimed. Her face lit up with such delight that the caretaker said she could keep two of them.

"One for me and one for Clara," she said, tucking them into her pockets.

Heidi found her way back home, and rang the doorbell. Sebastian came at once and whispered, "Come in quickly! They have all gone in to dinner—Miss Rottenmeier is furious!"

Heidi tried to slip into the dining room unnoticed, but Miss Rottenmeier said sternly, "Your behavior has been shocking, Heidi. You will be punished for leaving the house without permission and staying out so late. What do you have to say for yourself?"

"Meow!" came the surprising reply.

"Heidi!" shouted Miss Rottenmeier. "Do you dare to be rude on top of all your other misbehavior?"

"I'm not being rude," Heidi protested meekly.

"Meow! Meow!"

"This is too much!" cried Miss Rottenmeier, standing up. "Leave the room at once!" she said sternly.

"Please, Miss," Heidi begged, "it's not me. It's the kittens."

"Kittens?" screeched Miss Rottenmeier. "KITTENS? Sebastian! Come here at once and get rid of the horrible creatures!" She stormed out of the room.

By this time, both of the fluffy kittens were on Clara's lap and she and Heidi were playing with them.

"Sebastian, please help us," Clara said. "We want to keep the kittens and play with them whenever we can. Can you find a place to hide them?"

"Don't worry, Miss Clara," Sebastian replied. "I'll keep them in a basket in the attic. They'll be quite safe there."

The girls smiled happily at one another.

Grandmamma

Although Heidi was now good friends with Clara, she was still very homesick. She talked to Clara about Peter and the goats every day; and every day she said, "I must go home soon." She kept saving bread rolls for Peter's grandmother and was heartbroken when Miss Rottenmeier found them and threw them away.

One day, Clara told Heidi that her Grandmamma was coming to stay for a while. "Everyone loves her, and I'm sure you will too, Heidi," Clara said.

Clara was right. Grandmamma had a kind smile and merry, twinkling eyes. Heidi liked her at once. Every afternoon, while Clara was resting, Grandmamma sat with Heidi and read to her. One day, Grandmamma opened a book that had beautiful pictures of green fields where sheep and goats grazed. Looking at it, Heidi burst into loud sobs.

"You are missing the mountains, aren't you?" said Grandmamma, putting her arm around Heidi.

Heidi nodded miserably.

"When you can read this wonderful book for yourself, it shall be yours," Grandmamma promised.

Just a few days later, the Professor told Grandmamma that something astonishing had happened: Heidi could read! That evening at dinner time, Heidi found the beautiful book next to her plate.

"It is yours to keep forever," said Grandmamma with a twinkle in her eyes.

The House Is Haunted

When Grandmamma's visit ended, Heidi's homesickness got worse. She lost her appetite and grew very pale. Every night she cried herself to sleep.

One morning, the servants came downstairs to find the front door wide open. Thinking a thief had gotten in, they searched every corner of the house. Nothing was missing. When it happened again the next day, Sebastian said he would sit up that night to keep watch.

Just after midnight, Sebastian heard a loud *whoosh* as the front door was opened. He ran out and saw a ghostly figure in white disappearing up the stairs.

The next morning, all the servants were talking about the ghost. When Mr. Sesemann heard the story he invited Dr. Classen, the family doctor, to sit with him and wait for this "ghost" to appear.

That night, when the figure in white came downstairs to open the door, Mr. Sesemann and Dr. Classen were waiting for her. It was Heidi, walking in her sleep, looking just like a ghost.

"Dear child, what are you doing?" asked Mr. Sesemann softly, so as not to startle the girl.

Heidi's eyes flew open, and she looked confused. "I don't know," she said, beginning to cry.

The pale young girl told Dr. Classen about her sadness and how much she missed Grandfather and the Alm.

"There is only one thing to do," Dr. Classen told Mr. Sesemann later. "I'm afraid Heidi must go home."

Home to the Alm

The very next morning, Miss Rottenmeier was told to pack Heidi's things. Clara was very upset at losing her new friend, but her father promised her that they could visit Heidi the following summer.

After breakfast, Clara gave Heidi a basket of fresh, soft white rolls for Peter's grandmother. And Mr. Sesemann gave her an envelope for her grandfather.

"Be sure to keep it safe," he said kindly.

Sebastian took the train with Heidi all the way to Dörfli. There her trunk was put on a wagon to be delivered to Grandfather's hut. Heidi assured Sebastian she could walk up the mountain alone, which she did.

On her way up, Heidi stopped at Peter's cottage. Grandmother was overjoyed that Heidi was back. Heidi gave her the white rolls, saying, "Now you won't have to eat hard bread for a few days!"

Grandmother hugged her and said, "What blessings you bring! But the greatest blessing of all is you yourself."

After a while, Heidi continued her walk up the Alm. Before long, she could see the hut, and there, sitting on his bench and smoking his pipe, was Grandfather.

Heidi raced up and threw her arms around his neck, saying over and over, "Grandfather! Grandfather!" The old man's eyes filled with tears, and he hugged her as if he would never let her go.

"I've come home, Grandfather," said Heidi, "and I'm never going away again."

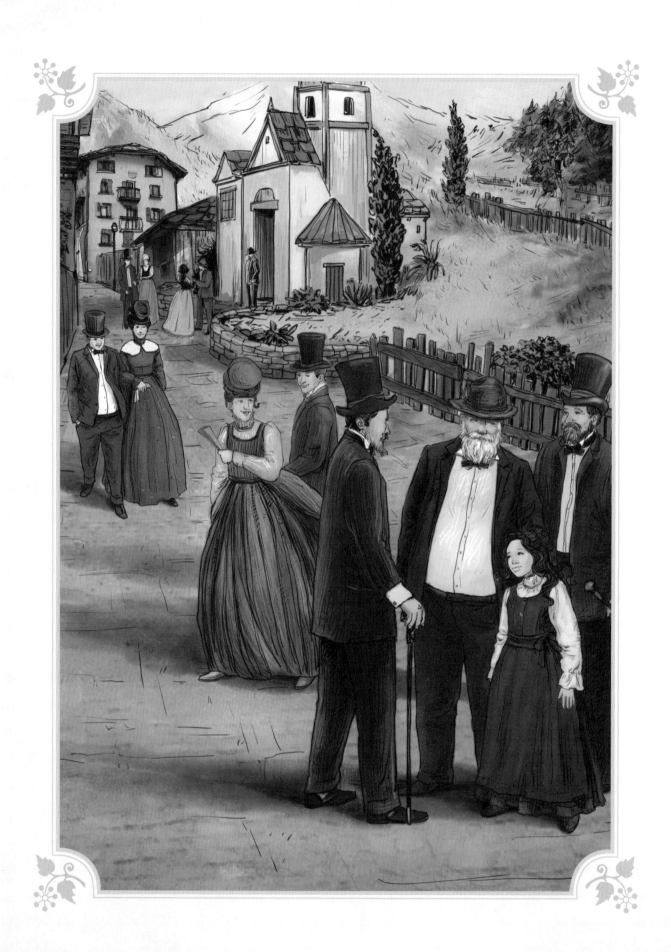

Heidi gave Grandfather the envelope from Mr. Sesemann. Inside there was a letter explaining why Heidi had come home, along with some money for her.

Grandfather wanted to use the money to buy Heidi a proper bed, but she said she would rather buy a soft white roll for Grandmother every morning.

Eager to show Grandfather how well she could read, Heidi took down a big Bible and read to him from it. Grandfather was pleased and proud, and as the next day was Sunday, he promised to take her to church in Dörfli.

So the next morning, as the church bells rang out from the village, Heidi and Grandfather walked down to Dörfli hand in hand. Everyone was surprised and happy to see Grandfather as he had not been to church for many years.

After the service, Grandfather stopped to talk to the pastor. "I have thought about your advice," he said, "and I realize now that you were right. I hope you will forgive me for being so stubborn. We will be moving down to Dörfli this winter so that Heidi can go to school."

As they left the church, many of the villagers crowded around to welcome Grandfather back to Dörfli. Heidi had never seen him smile so much. On their way home, Heidi and Grandfather stopped to tell Peter, his mother, and his grandmother the good news.

"I am glad you are back," said Peter.

"We will be going to school together," Heidi told Peter happily. "I can't wait!"

News for Clara

In Frankfurt, Clara was so looking forward to visiting Heidi. But as the summer drew near, Dr. Classen had some bad news for her.

"I'm afraid you're not strong enough to make the journey, my dear," the kind doctor told Clara and her father gently.

Choking back her sobs, Clara said, "Please, Dr. Classen, will you go instead?"

"But Clara, what will I do there?" the doctor asked in a surprised voice.

"Everything I would do!" exclaimed Clara. "You can meet Heidi's grandfather, and Peter and the goats, and then tell me all about it. And you can bring everyone the presents I have been saving for them. Please, Dr. Classen," she begged, grabbing the doctor's hand. "If you do, I promise to take all the cod liver oil you want me to, every day!" The doctor laughed.

"Well, if you promise that, I can hardly refuse, can I? When shall I go?"

"Tomorrow!" exclaimed Clara, smiling now.

Clara packed the presents very carefully: a warm woollen cape for Heidi; a cozy shawl and box of cakes for Peter's grandmother; some pipe tobacco for Heidi's grandfather; and delicious sausages for everyone. She couldn't wait to hear how Heidi liked her present. She would make sure the doctor told her everything!

Grandfather was in the shed, milking the goats, when Heidi rushed in, her face glowing with excitement.

"They're coming! Dr. Classen is coming! Clara and Grandmamma must be right behind him!" She turned and ran back to greet the guests from Frankfurt.

But when Dr. Classen arrived, he was all alone. Heidi was filled with disappointment when he explained why Clara and Grandmamma were not with him.

"Perhaps Clara will be well enough to come next spring," he told Heidi, not really believing it himself.

Grandfather welcomed the doctor with a hearty handshake and a delicious lunch of goat's milk, cheese, and cold meat.

"This is better than anything I have ever tasted in Frankfurt," Dr. Classen remarked.

Grandfather smiled proudly. "This is what Clara needs," he said. "Wholesome food and fresh mountain air would do wonders for the girl, I'm sure of it."

After lunch, a man delivered a large box—it was filled with the gifts from Clara. Heidi opened each present with a look of delight. The most exciting present of all was the box of cakes for Peter's grandmother.

"I want to take them to her right now!" said Heidi. As they all walked down the path to Peter's cottage, Heidi declared, "Nothing has made me happier than the doctor's visit."

Dr. Classen laughed, but inside he was deeply moved by Heidi's words.

School Days

In October, barely a month after Dr. Classen's visit, snow began falling on the mountain and Grandfather, Heidi, and the goats moved down to Dörfli. Grandfather had found an old, tumbledown house near the church, and had divided it into two sections, one for the goats and one for himself and Heidi. There was a big stove to keep the whole house warm and cozy, and there were lovely pictures on the walls for Heidi to look at.

Heidi started going to school, which she enjoyed very much. She knew that Peter came down to school on his sled, and she was looking forward to seeing him there. But Peter often stayed away from school, even on sunny days when it would have been easy for him to get there.

"Why don't you come to school more often?" Heidi asked him one day. Peter was embarrassed and didn't want to answer at first.

"I have never learned to read," he finally confessed. "And so I find school difficult."

"You can learn," Heidi told him. "I can teach you."

Peter grumbled, but Heidi convinced him that he would be able to do it. She started by teaching him the alphabet, just as the Professor had done in Frankfurt.

Peter started coming to school more regularly, and every afternoon he sat with Heidi learning new letters and words. By the middle of the winter, Peter was able to read to his grandmother from her hymn book, which made her very happy indeed.

A Letter

The winter in Dörfli passed happily for Heidi. Before she knew it, May had arrived, and the mountain streams, fed by all the melted snow, rushed and leaped down into the valley. It was time for Heidi and Grandfather to go back to their home high on the Alm.

Heidi ran everywhere, looking for new wild flowers in the grass, feeling the warm sun on her cheeks, and listening to the wind rushing through the pines. She hadn't realized how much she had missed everything.

Peter was back too, looking after the goats. They too were pleased to be on the mountain, grazing on the new green grass. Heidi rushed out to meet Peter every morning, happy that they would be spending carefree days together again.

One morning, Peter had something for Heidi. "The postmaster gave me this to give to you," he said. It was from Clara! Excited, Heidi ran to read it to Grandfather.

"Dear Heidi," the letter began. "We are coming to see you! We hope to come in six weeks, after I have had some treatments. Father needs to be in Paris, but Grandmamma will be with me. I can hardly wait!"

Heidi was relieved to read that Miss Rottenmeier would be staying in Frankfurt. The letter was signed, "Your true friend, Clara".

Heidi thought she would burst with happiness. Clara would be coming to her mountain at last!

Then one day in June, Heidi saw a strange procession winding its way up the Alm. Two men were carrying a wheelchair on poles, and in the chair sat Clara, well wrapped in blankets and shawls. Behind her was Grandmamma, on horseback.

"They're here!" cried Heidi, rushing to get Grandfather. Together they made their way down to greet their guests.

As Clara's chair was gently set down, she gazed about in wonder. "It's so beautiful!" she said. "I wish I could run around and see everything with you, Heidi!"

"I'll show it all to you," said Heidi. She pushed Clara's chair to the pines, so that Clara could hear the wind rushing through them. Then she took Clara to see her favorite goats, Little Swan and Little Bear, in their stalls. At lunchtime, Grandmamma couldn't believe how the fresh mountain air had given Clara such a good appetite. Later that day, Heidi showed Clara and Grandmamma her bed in the sweet-smelling hayloft.

"What a wonderful bedroom you have!" exclaimed Clara. "The hay looks so soft, and the blue sky is right outside your window."

"If Grandmamma agrees," said Grandfather, "we would be very happy for you stay for a few weeks."

Grandmamma smiled. "I think it would do her good," she said. "And I thank you with all my heart."

Heidi and Clara beamed at one another, and started planning all the things they would do together.

The next morning, Heidi and Clara sat outside the hut. Clara breathed in the scent of the pine trees—she already felt better than she had in Frankfurt.

Grandfather brought out mugs of fresh, creamy milk for the girls. "This is from Little Swan," he said. "Drink up, Clara. It will give you strength!"

Soon Peter arrived, expecting Heidi to join him.

"Clara is here, so I can't come today," she explained, "or tomorrow or the day after. Grandfather has said that he might take both of us up to the pasture one day, but for now I am staying here with Clara."

Peter scowled, but said nothing. He turned and drove the goats up the mountain as fast as he could, never once looking back.

Heidi and Clara had promised to write to Grandmamma every day, so Heidi brought out everything they needed from the house and they wrote their letters in the warm sunshine.

Grandfather said that Clara needed lots of sunshine and fresh air. After lunch, Heidi took Clara's chair to a shady spot under a tree, where the warm breeze ruffled their hair.

They spent the afternoon telling each other everything that had happened since they had last seen each other.

As the sun began to sink, Heidi saw Peter bringing the goats down and called to him. But he did not answer or even turn his head.

A Present from Grandmamma

Over the next few weeks, Grandfather took Clara out in her chair every morning, and she and Heidi spent the day outdoors. And every morning Grandfather said to Clara kindly, "Will you try to stand today?"

To please him, Clara always tried, holding his arm for support. "Oh, it hurts!" she would cry. But every day, Grandfather gently encouraged her to stand for a few seconds longer.

The girls had breakfast and lunch outdoors. Clara loved the goat's milk Grandfather gave them, and she drank hers even more quickly than Heidi did.

With all the fresh air and good food, Clara slept very well at night, and always woke up happy and well rested. One day, the girls saw two men coming up the mountain, each carrying a bed on his back. They also had fresh white sheets and blankets and pillows—and a letter from Grandmamma.

The letter said that the beds were for Heidi and Clara. Heidi was to take hers to the house in Dörfli so she would be warm in winter, and Clara's could stay in Grandfather's hut ready for her next visit.

Grandfather cleared the hay from the hayloft, and helped the men take the beds up the ladder to the loft. He placed them perfectly, so both girls could see equally well out of the window.

"From now on, we shall both sleep in proper beds!" said Heidi joyfully, and the two girls laughed.

First Steps

One bright morning, Grandfather agreed to take both girls up to the pasture where Peter grazed the goats. He brought Clara's wheelchair outside, then went back into the hut to fetch the girls.

At that very moment, Peter came by. Ever since Clara had arrived and taken Heidi away from him, Peter had felt angry. When he saw Clara's wheelchair, his anger burst out and he pushed the chair as hard as he could, smiling grimly as he watched it tumble down the mountainside and shatter into pieces.

Grandfather wondered what had happened to the chair, but he assured the girls that they could still go up to the pasture. He carried Clara there, placing her gently on a blanket on the sunny grass next to Heidi. When Peter saw them, he scowled and turned away.

"I wish you could see the wild flowers, Clara," Heidi said a while later. "Maybe Peter and I can carry you over to look at them."

Peter still wanted nothing to do with Clara, but when he saw that she really could not stand, he felt sorry for what he had done, and agreed to help her. Together, Heidi and Peter managed to get Clara to stand. Then Heidi gently coaxed her to take a step.

"It hurts," Clara said, "but not as much as it used to!" Bravely, Clara took another step, and another. "Heidi, look!" she cried. "I can do it! I can walk!"

Grandmamma was coming to fetch Clara in a week's time, and every day for the next week, Grandfather and Heidi helped Clara take a few more steps.

When Grandmamma finally arrived, she could hardly recognize Clara. "Your cheeks are so round and rosy!" she exclaimed. "And where is your chair?"

In reply, Heidi helped Clara to stand. Together, they walked to Grandmamma, their faces beaming.

Grandmamma gasped. Then, laughing and crying at the same time, she embraced Clara with joy.

The next day, there was a big surprise for Clara—her father arrived from Paris! When he saw his daughter walking toward him, he was too overcome to speak. He folded Clara in his arms, and kissed her again and again.

"We can never thank you and Heidi enough," Mr. Sesemann told Grandfather later. "Tell me your dearest wish, and it shall be yours."

Grandfather said his reward was seeing Clara grow so healthy but Heidi asked that Peter's grandmother have her bed from Frankfurt. She wanted her to be warm during the winter.

Sadly it was time to say goodbye. The girls hugged, and Clara promised she would be back next summer.

Heidi waved to her friends until they were out of sight. Then she took her grandfather's hand and together they walked home, both happy and content. Heidi's kindness had brought joy to so many people, but she had transformed her grandfather's life most of all.

THE END

An Imprint of Sterling Publishing
1166 Avenue of The Americas
New York, NY, 10036

SANDY CREEK and the distinctive Sandy Creek logo are registered trademarks of Barnes & Noble, Inc.

Text © 2016 by QEB Publishing, Inc.
Illustrations © 2016 by QEB Publishing, Inc.

This 2016 edition published by Sandy Creek.

All rights reserved. No part of this publication may be reproduced, stored in a retrieval system
or transmitted in any form or by any means (including electronic, mechanical, photocopying, recording,
or otherwise) without prior written permission from the publisher.

ISBN 978-1-4351-6329-4

Manufactured in Guangdong, China
Lot #:
4 6 8 10 9 7 5 3 2 1
02/16